THE EDGE OF DESTRUCTION

DOCTOR WHO
THE EDGE OF DESTRUCTION

based on the BBC television series by David Whitaker
by arrangement with BBC Books, a division of BBC Enterprises Ltd

NIGEL ROBINSON

Number 132 in the
Doctor Who Library

A TARGET BOOK
published by
the Paperback Division of
W. H. ALLEN & Co. Plc

A Target Book
Published in 1988
By the Paperback Division of
W. H. Allen & Co. Plc
44 Hill Street, London W1X 8LB

First published in Great Britain by
W. H. Allen & Co. Plc, 1988

The BBC producers of *The Edge of Destruction* were Verity Lambert
and Mervyn Pinfold
The directors were Richard Martin and Frank Cox
The role of the Doctor was played by William Hartnell

Printed and bound in Great Britain by
Cox & Wyman Ltd, Reading

ISBN 0 426 20327 5

Contents

Introduction

It all started, they would say later, in a forgotten London junkyard on a foggy November night in 1963. But in truth, for Ian Chesterton and Barbara Wright it had started some five months earlier.

It had all begun with fifteen-year-old Susan Foreman who had just joined the school. From the start Susan had proved something of a mystery. Despite five months' constant nagging from Miss Johnson, the school secretary, she was still unable to produce a birth certificate or indeed any other documentation to prove her status; neither was her grandfather, with whom she lived, on the electoral register of Coal Hill or any other London district.

She had just returned from a long stay abroad, Susan explained, and the necessary papers were still in transit. Miss Johnson had thought of telephoning the girl's grandfather but he was not listed in the phone directory; the two letters she wrote to him remained unanswered. Fortunately Miss Johnson was a mild-mannered woman, not the normal stuff of school secretaries, and as the months passed she began to despair of ever completing her file on Susan Foreman.

Looking at Susan, Barbara Wright could believe that the girl had spent most of her life abroad. Her speech was clear and precise, as though English was not her mother tongue, or at least she was unused to speaking it.

7

Occasionally she would use a word or phrase in her conversation which, although not technically wrong, was unsuitable, just as if she had learnt English from a text book. When she spoke, however, it was with a peculiar lilt which was not unattractive.

She often seemed nervous in the presence of her fellow pupils, as if she was uncertain of their customs, and though she was a pleasant enough girl she seemed to have few friends at school; those pupils she did associate with appeared rather in awe of her.

The one time Barbara had asked Susan about her background the girl had just smiled sweetly and said, 'We travelled around quite a lot when I was a child.' But Susan's large almond eyes, finely-boned cheeks and slightly Oriental complexion suggested that she had some Asiatic blood in her.

As history teacher, Barbara Wright had a special interest in Susan. Most of Barbara's pupils regarded history as a dull chore, especially when it was the last lesson on a Friday afternoon. But Susan greeted each lesson with genuine enthusiasm. She was passionately interested in every period of history and at times displayed a knowledge of certain ages which astounded even Barbara. Barbara recognised in Susan a potential university candidate and offered to work with her at home; but Susan had firmly refused, giving as an excuse the fact that her grandfather did not welcome strangers.

Ian Chesterton, the handsome young science master, had been having similar problems. Susan's marks for her written papers were consistently excellent – surprisingly so for a girl of her age – but in class she seemed strangely detached, as though Ian's practical demonstrations of physics and chemistry simply bored her.

Even the spectacular experiments Ian reserved for Monday morning, in a futile attempt to gain his pupils' jaded post-weekend enthusiasm, failed to excite her spirits. At these times Susan seemed different from the rest of the class, a girl apart.

But if Susan was extraordinarily good at science and history, she was unbelievably bad at other subjects. Her geography was laughable, and her knowledge of English literature at best patchy: she could quote, for example, huge chunks of Shakespearean verse but had never even heard of Charles Dickens, let alone read any of his works. However, her foreign languages – French, Latin and the optional Ancient Greek – were surprisingly fluent for a schoolgirl, a fact Barbara put down to her having lived abroad and acquired an ear for languages.

In short, Susan Foreman was a problem child. And so it was on a foggy Friday night in November that Ian and Barbara resolved to visit the girl's guardian and discuss her erratic performance at school. Miss Johnson gave them her address – 76 Totters Lane – and they drove there in Ian's battered old Volkswagen. It was a journey that changed their lives forever.

76 Totters Lane was far from what Ian and Barbara had expected. They had imagined it to be a rather dilapidated terraced house in a slightly run-down area of London; instead it was nothing more than a junkyard. There, surrounded by the clutter of unwanted pieces of furniture, and discarded bicycles and knickknacks, was, of all things, a police telephone box, similar to many which stood on London street corners at that time. But like 76 Totters Lane this police telephone box was not what it seemed.

Even years later in their old age Barbara and Ian would never forget that first thrill of disbelief as they entered that out-of-place police box. Instead of the cramped darkened space they expected to find beyond the double doors, they crossed the threshold into a spacious, brilliantly lit futuristic control room whose dimensions totally contradicted its outside appearance. Standing in the middle of the impossibly huge control control chamber, astonished to see them, was Susan Foreman.

And there Ian and Barbara finally met their problem pupil's grandfather, a tall imperious septuagenarian with a flowing mane of white hair and a haughty demeanour which suffered no fools gladly. Dressed in a crisp wing collar shirt and cravat and the dark frock-coat of an Edwardian family solicitor he seemed to the teachers to be not of their time, an anachronism from another point in history all together.

As indeed he was. For Susan and the man they were to come to know as the Doctor were aliens, beings from another planet unimaginable light years and countless centuries away from the Earth of 1963. The machine in which they were standing was the TARDIS, a philosopher's dream come true, a craft capable of crossing the boundaries of all space and all time, and of bending all the proven laws of physics.

Suspicious of the true intentions of the two teachers and wary that if they were allowed to leave they would reveal his and Susan's presence on their planet, the Doctor had activated his machine and taken all of them to prehistoric Earth. There they were captured by a group of savage cavemen and nearly sacrificed to their god. It was the courage and resourcefulness of Ian and

Barbara which saw them through that crisis and returned them safely to the TARDIS.

Having won the Doctor's grudging respect – if not yet his friendship – the two teachers demanded that he take them back to their own time. But mental giant though he undoubtedly was, even the Doctor did not understand fully the complexities of the TARDIS; and so it was that their next journey took them not to Earth but to the desolate radiation-soaked world of Skaro in the distant future. There they encountered the deadly Daleks and once again the Doctor displayed his distrust of all other creatures but his granddaughter Susan, at one point even going so far as callously to suggest abandoning Barbara in order to leave the planet safely. Ian had vetoed that suggestion and the four time-travellers finally survived their ordeals and returned to the TARDIS.

But as Ian and Barbara left the planet Skaro they began to realise that the chances of them ever seeing their home world again were very slim. Their entire fates were in the hands of an irascible old man whom they did not understand and whom they still did not trust.

The vicissitudes of his character were a constant puzzle to them; at one moment he could be generous and caring to a fault, the next he was a selfish old man whose only concern was the safety of himself and his granddaughter. And now that they knew of her origins even Susan's behaviour appeared disconcerting and unpredictable.

Indeed, it seemed to them that the only thing remaining constant and unchanging throughout their travels was the TARDIS itself, running with the

11

emotionless, unthinking precision of a well-conditioned if slightly erratic machine.

But they were wrong, far more wrong than they could ever have realised. For the TARDIS was more – much, much more – than a mere machine . . .

Prologue

The tall glass column in the centre of the six-sided central control console rose and fell with a stately elegance, indicating that the TARDIS was in full flight. Around the console, the Doctor fussed with the controls, adjusting this dial and checking that read-out from the on-board computer.

As at all similar times he was oblivious of his companions, his only thought being to guide the TARDIS through the hazardous lanes of the time vortex and back out into the universe of real time-space. Beside him his companions watched with rapt fascination.

Ian and Barbara looked on, not quite knowing what the Doctor was doing but impressed by his seeming facility at and mastery of the complex controls. Susan had seen this procedure many times before but even she felt a sense of awe as the old man drove home the final levers on the control panels.

The Doctor stood back from the console, a satisfied gleam in his eyes, and flexed his hands, as a pianist would after a particularly long and difficult piece. Suddenly his brow furrowed and, worried, he bent forward over the controls. His companions noticed his sudden concern but there was no time to remark upon it.

A tremendous crash resounded throughout the control chamber, deafening them, and the floor itself began to vibrate beneath their feet with stomach-churning violence. They staggered away from the console as the shuddering increased, knocking them off-balance and throwing them into the walls and the pieces of antique furniture which littered the room.

At the same time a searing white light burst out from the central column. Instinctively they all covered their eyes. So intense was the light that for one appalling moment their bones were visible through the skin of their outstretched hands.

A massive charge of power circulated throughout the entire room, a charge so powerful that their feeble nervous systems could not cope with it and unconsciousness descended mercifully upon each one of them.

The blaze of light from the column slowly faded to an insignificant glimmer. All around the four senseless bodies lights flickered and faltered and then faded altogether, until much of the control room was in darkness; only a few emergency lights provided any sort of illumination. A thin shaft of light beamed down on the control console and on the glass column which had now fallen to a halt.

The TARDIS was deadly silent. The constant humming of the motors and machinery, and the clatter of the banks of computers, had all ceased. The only noise to be heard was the soft and irregular breathing of the Doctor, Susan, Ian and Barbara, as they lay, struggling to hold on to life, unconscious and helpless on the floor of the time-machine.

1

Aftershock

The school bell woke Barbara up. She slowly opened her eyes and looked around, annoyed at herself for having fallen asleep once again during one of the few free periods she had in her timetable. She ought to be up and about, marking essays and preparing classes, she reminded herself, not dozing off in one of the comfortable armchairs in the staff room of Coal Hill School.

But as she gathered her thoughts together, she excused herself on the grounds that today had been an exceptionally busy day. For a start she had had to fill in for Mr Lamb, the German master, who was taking a party of schoolchildren on a study trip to the Black Forest. After that she had had a difficult period with Class 4B for whom the American War of Independence had been just a good excuse to start an ink pellet battle.

She looked anxiously at her watch and then breathed a sigh of relief. She still had another forty minutes before her class on the Aztecs of fifteenth-century South America, ample time to think of some way to grab the interest of less than enthusiastic pupils. She glanced across the staff room at Ian Chesterton and allowed herself a small smile as she saw that he too was slumped in a chair fast asleep.

Suddenly she started. Ian shouldn't be asleep; didn't he have a class right now?

If the headmaster found he had missed a class because he was having forty winks there would be all hell to pay. Still slightly groggy with sleep Barbara stood up and crossed over to the slumbering science teacher.

'Mr Chesterton?' she said, shaking him gently by the shoulders. 'Ian, wake up.' But Ian merely muttered and carried on sleeping.

Barbara turned around sharply as she registered the presence of another person, standing at the other end of the room. She was about to reprove the girl for entering the staff room without knocking when she saw her pale expression. Barbara's natural sympathy went out to her and she rushed over to her. The girl was obviously in some distress.

'It's Susan Foreman, isn't it?' she said.

The girl nodded vaguely and then put her hand to her temple and moaned. She seemed on the verge of fainting and Barbara supported her by the arm. 'Have you hurt your head?' she asked.

Susan nodded again. 'Yes, it's terrible.' There was no visible wound but Susan began to massage her temple to ease away the evident pain she was feeling.

'Let me look at it,' urged Barbara, but Susan seemed to only half-hear.

'My leg hurts too,' she said, and bent down to rub her knee. Barbara led her to a chair. As she slumped into it, Susan sighed.

'That's better, the pain's gone now . . .' She looked around the staff room in a daze, blinked, and then some sort of comprehension seemed to dawn in her face. 'For a moment I couldn't think where I was . . .'

Barbara looked at her oddly and was about to question her further when Susan saw the body of the old

16

man on the floor. She leapt out of her chair. '*Grand-father!*' she cried and dashed over to him.

For the first time Barbara registered the presence of the old man, and for one ludicrous moment felt slightly annoyed that he had chosen the middle of the staff room in which to keel over. Then she too darted over to his side and bent over him in concern.

She looked at him curiously, not quite recognising his face; but her practical mind supposed he was one of the assistant teachers employed to stand in for those members of staff who had been laid off by the flu which was going around the area at the moment. He looked as though he might be a Latin or Religious teacher. There was a particularly nasty wound on the side of his head, and his long silver-white hair was flecked with blood.

'He's cut his head open,' she said.

Susan suddenly took charge. 'I've got some ointment.'

'Good,' approved Barbara. 'And get some water too.'

Susan stood up and headed for the door, and Barbara watched her as she passed the large table in the centre of the staff room. Suddenly Susan moaned in dismay as an overwhelming dizziness overcame her. Barbara watched her stagger away from the table.

'Susan, what is it?' she cried out, and made to go after her.

Susan steadied herself and waved aside Barbara's offer of assistance. She seemed to have forgotten the old man lying on the floor and was instead pointing at the figure of Ian slumped in his chair.

'Shouldn't we go and help him?' she asked.

What was the girl talking about? thought Barbara irately. Ian was only asleep after all; the way Susan was going on you'd have thought he was on his last legs!

'Don't be silly, Susan,' she snapped. 'Mr Chesterton is perfectly all right.' She turned her attention to the old man. 'But I don't like the look of this cut at all . . .'

Susan suddenly remembered. 'Oh yes . . .' she said slowly. 'Water . . .' And then in a quizzical voice: 'What happened?'

'I don't know!' Barbara replied tetchily. 'Just do as you're told!'

With that, Susan left the room. Barbara took off her cardigan and laid it underneath the old man's head. Satisfied that he was comfortable, she walked over to Ian who had unbelievably slept through the entire crisis. This time she managed to shake him awake.

He looked groggily at her. 'You're working late to-night, Miss Wright . . .' he said, and then raised a head to his aching forehead. For one moment he thought he might have had one drink too many at The Cricketers, the pub many of the teaching staff frequented after school hours.

'Don't be stupid, Ian,' Barbara said. 'It's the middle of the afternoon – and you've missed your physics class,' she continued as an added reproof.

Ian winced at being once more on the receiving end of one of Barbara's reprimands. He attempted to stand up and promptly sat down again as the world spun sickenly around him. He groaned; perhaps he had spent his lunchtime at The Cricketers after all.

'Do you think I could have a glass of water, Barbara?' he asked.

'Susan's getting some.'

'Susan?'

'Yes, Susan Foreman.'

Still dazed, Ian looked around the staff room and saw the old man. 'What's he doing there?' he asked slowly.

'He's cut his head,' Barbara explained. 'There's nothing we can do until Susan gets back with the water and ointment.'

But Ian had already crossed over the staff room – with some difficulty – and was kneeling by the old man. He felt his chest and looked up at Barbara with relief.

'His heart's all right and his breathing's quite regular.' He brushed away the locks of white hair to examine the cut more closely. 'I don't think that cut's as bad as you seem to think it is either.'

'But what if his skull's fractured?'

Ian gave a wry grin: Barbara was fussing too much again. 'I don't think it's as bad as all that,' he repeated. 'But who is he?'

Barbara frowned. 'Don't you know? I thought he was one of the replacement teachers . . .'

Ian shook his head. 'I've never seen the old boy in my life before.'

Barbara was about to speak when the old man began to stir. His lips trembled and he muttered something. Bending down, Ian and Barbara could just make out his words.

'I can't take you back, Susan . . . I can't!' he groaned and then seemed to slip back into unconsciousness.

Barbara and Ian exchanged curious looks. What was the old man talking about? Ian shrugged. 'He's rambling,' he said.

But something in the old man's tone and his reference to Susan had struck a chord in Barbara's mind. She blinked and looked around her.

What her tired and shocked brain had rationalised as

19

the staff room of Coal Hill school now shattered into a million shimmering pieces of light and reformed itself. The walls, she saw, were covered with large circular indentations, not staff notices as she had thought. The staff television set, positioned high on a shelf, was now a much stranger-looking video screen flush with the wall itself. Even the large table where most of the staff did their marking shrunk and transformed itself into a strange mushroom-shaped console.

Finally recovered from the shock of the massive discharge of energy her brain at last correcly translated the images from her surroundings. She clutched Ian's arm, her attentions temporarily turned away from the unconscious form of the Doctor.

'Ian, look! Can't you see?'

Ian frowned as, prompted by Barbara, his own surroundings began to redefine themselves. 'What is it?' he asked, still a little dazed.

The memories came flooding back, as everything began to make sense. 'It's the Ship,' said Barbara, almost wonderingly. 'We're in the TARDIS!'

Although still dazed from her shock, and confused by Barbara's strange manner, for Susan the TARDIS was home, and she recognised it for what it was practically as soon as she came to. So it was easy for her to find her way out of the control room and down one of the several corridors which led off it into the interior of the Ship.

The one she followed took her to a small utility room adjacent to the living quarters. There she went to a first-aid cabinet and took out a roll of striped bandage, from which she cut off a length with a pair of scissors. She put the bandage in one of the large pockets of her dress, and absent-mindedly put the scissors in there too.

Remembering the water, she walked over into the TARDIS rest room. This was a large chamber about the size of the control room which she and her grandfather, and latterly Ian and Barbara, used for recreation and relaxation. A large bookcase dominated one entire wall of the room, containing first editions of all the great classics of Earth literature: the Complete Works of Shakespeare (some of which were personally signed); *Le Contrat Social* of Rousseau; Plato's *The Republic*; and a peculiar work by a French philosopher called Fontenelle on the possibility of life on other planets (that one had always made the Doctor chuckle). Susan's English teacher at Coal Hill would have been interested to note that there was nothing by Charles Dickens in the Doctor's library.

There were several items of antique furniture in the room, none as austere as those in the control room. Looking out of place by a magnificent Chippendale *chaise-longue* and a mahogany table, on which stood an ivory backgammon set, was the food machine – a large bank of dials and buttons, similar to a soft-drinks dispenser on Earth. Susan tapped out the code on the keyboard which would supply water.

She frowned as the LED showed that the machine was empty. However, a plastic sachet of water was nevertheless produced. Confused, Susan shrugged, collected the sachet, and made her way back to the control room.

Susan ran all the way back, anxious not to let a minute be wasted in treating her grandfather. But when she reached the control chamber she stood stock still, frozen in horror, all thoughts of her grandfather temporarily banished from her mind.

Barbara and Ian were still bent over the unconscious form of the Doctor, but they leapt to their feet instantly when they heard Susan's cry of terror. They followed Susan's finger as it pointed, trembling, at the double doors behind them.

Soundlessly they were opening, flooding the control room with a bright, unearthly light. Beyond that light the three travellers could see nothing – just a white, gaping void.

Unable to move, Susan managed to say in a terrified whisper: 'The doors . . . they can't open on their own . . . They can't . . .'

And then her voice faded away, as she looked at the control console still bathed in an overhead shaft of light. The central time rotor was stationary, a normal indication that the TARDIS had landed. But the few displays which were still operational clearly showed that the time-machine was still in flight.

And if that was so, reasoned Susan, all three of them should have been blasted to atoms the very second the exit doors opened and let in the furious uncontrollable forces of the time vortex. And less importantly, but even more curiously, the door controls on the console were still in the locked mode.

By rights the doors should not be open; and by rights they should all be dead. What was happening to the TARDIS?

Ian gestured vaguely over to the figure of the Doctor on the floor. 'Perhaps he opened the doors before he cut his head open?' he suggested. 'Perhaps there was some

22

kind of a fault, a delayed reaction, and they've only just opened?'

Susan looked down at her grandfather but made no move towards him. 'No . . . he wouldn't . . . not while we were in flight . . .' Her voice was weak and tremulous.

'Then they must have been forced open when we crashed,' said Barbara.

'Crashed?' asked Ian.

'Yes, Ian, try and remember. There was an explosion and then we all passed out.'

'No,' said Susan firmly. 'The Ship can't crash – at least not in the way you mean. It's impossible . . . And anyway, the controls say we're still in flight . . .' Her voice tailed off again, and then after a short pause: 'Listen.'

'Listen to what, Susan?' asked Ian. 'There's nothing to hear.'

The girl nodded. 'That's right . . . Everything's stopped. Everything's as silent as . . . as . . .' In the shadowy, eerie surroundings of the control room she could not bring herself to say the word 'grave'.

'No,' said Barbara. 'There *is* something. Listen . . .'

As their ears strained to do so, they heard a series of long drawn-out sighs, in-out in-out in-out, like the sound of a wounded man trying to catch his last breaths before dying. In the darkness it sounded ominous and frightening.

Barbara shuddered. It must be the life support system of the TARDIS pumping oxygen into the Ship, she reasoned; it *had* to be . . .

Susan looked around the control room. The light from the open doors illuminated the faces of her two

23

teachers with a ghastly brilliance, making their features unreal and ghoulish. Other lights cast uncanny shadows on the walls; the shadow of the Doctor's eagle-shaped lectern threatened them like a nightmarish bird of prey. The shaft of brightness over the control console grew stronger and then fainter, and then stronger again, as if it were pulsing in time to the all-pervasive breathing sound. Susan raised a hand to her forehead and discovered she had broken out into a cold sweat.

Barbara came forward to comfort her. 'Susan, it's all right.'

Susan shrugged herself free of the schoolteacher's touch. 'No,' she insisted, her eyes darting in all directions, 'you're wrong. I've got a feeling about this. There's something *inside* the Ship!'

'That's not possible,' said Ian with more conviction than he was beginning to feel in the circumstances.

'You feel it, don't you?' Susan asked Barbara, almost accusingly.

Barbara felt a shiver run down her spine, but was determined not to let her fear show. 'Now, don't be silly, Susan,' she chided and pointed over to the Doctor on the floor. 'Your grandfather's ill.'

'What?'

Barbara looked strangely at her former pupil. This was not the way she normally acted. At any other time she would have been at her grandfather's side in an instant. But instead she seemed to be looking glassy-eyed into the distance; the shock of the crash – or whatever it was – must have affected her more than she had imagined. Even Ian seemed more lethargic and quieter than usual.

'Susan, snap out of it!' she said sternly. 'Give me the

24

bandage.'

Shaken out of her trance, Susan handed the bandage over to Barbara who looked quizzically at the multi-coloured stripes on the fabric.

'The coloured part is the ointment,' explained Susan. 'You'll find that the colour disappears as it goes into the wound. When the bandage is white the wound is completely healed.'

Barbara nodded approvingly and bent down to the Doctor again. After mopping his brow with her handkerchief and the water Susan had brought, she wrapped the bandage around his head. She couldn't resist a small chuckle; with the multi-coloured bandage around his head, the Doctor looked just like a pirate.

While the two girls had been tending to the Doctor Ian had sauntered over to the open doors. He was determined to see what – if anything – might lie outside. When he got to within three feet of them, they closed with a resounding *thud!*, plunging the control room once more into semi-darkness. Barbara and Susan looked up at the noise, as Ian turned around to face them.

'Did you do that?' he asked urgently.

'We haven't moved.' Susan tried hard to keep her voice steady, but the fear she felt was apparent. 'Neither of us has touched the controls.'

Ian turned and moved away from the doors and back towards his two companions. As he did so, the doors swung open again, bathing the control room once more in an unearthly light. He spun round and began to walk smartly back to the doors which, as he approached them, thudded shut one more.

'What's going on here?' he asked irately. 'Are you

25

playing a game with me?'

The two girls shook their heads. Susan looked particularly distraught. The Doctor and the TARDIS were the only two things in her life which had proved constant and true; and now her grandfather lay unconscious on the floor, and the TARDIS was beginning to behave with an almost malevolent unpredictability. If those two things failed her what would she have left?

Suddenly she shook herself out of her uncertainty and sprang to her feet. With the Doctor out of action she was the only one who could possibly discover what was happening to the TARDIS.

'I'm going to try the controls,' she resolved.

Barbara muttered a word of caution but Susan strode resolutely over to the central control console. She reached out a hand to touch the controls on one of the six panels but before she could, her body convulsed, her back arched, and she fell away from the controls to join her grandfather unconscious on the floor.

Ian rushed to her side, and felt automatically for a pulse. He looked over to Barbara. 'She's fainted,' he said. 'But I don't understand it – she was perfectly all right a minute ago.'

'Yes,' said Barbara. 'But a while before that you were all unconscious . . .'

Ian stood up and moved to the control console. As he did so he staggered and seemed about to fall. Barbara was at his side in an instant.

'What is it?' she asked, her voice full of concern.

Ian shook his head. 'I don't know . . . I suddenly felt dizzy . . .' He raised a hand to his brow. 'And I've got this terrible headache . . .'

'That's not like you at all . . .' said Barbara. Nor-

26

mally Ian was in the best of health. 'You don't think it could be radiation sickness, do you? Like we had on Skaro?'

'I don't know, Barbara,' Ian replied helplessly. 'We don't know what power that explosion may have unleashed . . .'

'Sit down,' urged Barbara. 'Let me help you to a chair.'

As they moved away from the console, Ian pointed to the doors. This time they had remained closed.

'I don't understand it,' he said. 'What is going on around here? How could those doors have opened by themselves?'

'Ian, you don't think something could have taken over the TARDIS, do you?' Barbara could still hear the steady in-out in-out breathing all around them; logic told her it was the TARDIS's life support systems – but in the threatening gloom of the control chamber she was not too sure. Had an intruder somehow come aboard the TARDIS and was even now stalking them?

'How am I supposed to know!' snapped Ian and then immediately apologised for his sharp tone; the tension and uncertainty of their situation were beginning to affect him too.

By their feet the Doctor began to groan. Barbara bent down to tend to him. 'He's beginning to stir,' she said, and then looked at Ian in concern. 'Ian, are you feeling better now?' Ian said he was. 'Well, take Susan and put her to bed. I'll look after the Doctor.'

Ian nodded, and picked up Susan gently in his arms. As he left the room he turned for one final look at Barbara kneeling in concern over the frail figure of the old man. 'If anything happens, let me know.'

Barbara smiled, a half-hearted smile which did nothing to conceal the anxiety she felt. 'What could happen?' she asked.

'I don't know . . .' said Ian, and realised that in this ignorance lay their greatest weakness. If they knew what they were up against they could approach it rationally and conquer it. But in the darkness and silence of a strangely threatening TARDIS all they had was their fear of the unknown, a fear which was already tearing their nerves to shreds.

As Ian left the room, the Doctor's eyelids fluttered open. He looked up glassy-eyed at Barbara's face. It seemed to take several moments for him to recognise her. And when he did his first concern was for his granddaughter.

'Susan,' he croaked through dry lips. 'Is Susan all right?'

Barbara smiled reassuringly down at him. 'She's fine. Ian's taking care of her right now. But how are you?'

Satisfied that his granddaughter was well, the Doctor breathed a sigh of relief and allowed himself to examine his own condition. With the schoolteacher's help he managed to sit up. 'My head . . .' he complained and felt the bandage.

'You cut your forehead when you fell,' explained Barbara. 'But you'll be all right; the ointment is working its way it.' The coloured stripes on the bandage were much paler than before, a sure sign that Susan's treatment was working.

The Doctor massaged the back of his neck. 'It hurts here,' he complained.

Barbara examined the old man's neck; she could see no sign of a lump or a bruise. As she looked, the Doctor let out a sigh of terrible anguish.

Barbara was shaken: she had never seen the Doctor like this before. For the first time she realised how much they all depended on him and how central he had become to all their lives; if anything were to happen to him there was no telling how they would ever escape from the madhouse the TARDIS seemed to have become. Would Susan, a mere child, be able to operate the Ship's controls by herself? Barbara knew that she and Ian certainly couldn't.

Looking into the deep impenetrable shadows which shrouded the control room, and listening to that laboured in-out in-out breathing, Barbara was suddenly worried and very, very scared . . .

Ian carried Susan's limp body down shadowy corridors until he reached the TARDIS's sleeping quarters. As always, he wondered at the sheer size of the time-machine. Its corridors and passageways seemed to wind on forever and he knew that during his short time on board the Doctor's Ship he had only explored a small fraction of them.

In fact, all he had seen of the TARDIS was the control room and the living, sleeping and recreational areas. There was no telling what else might be hidden deep inside the time-machine.

The Doctor and Susan had talked of a laboratory and a workshop, even of a conservatory and a private art gallery and studio, but the Doctor actively discouraged further exploration of his ship. Even after long weeks of travelling together and their ordeals on prehistoric Earth and on Skaro he still did not quite trust the two schoolteachers who had forced their presence upon him

29

in Totters Lane.

Suspicious and ungrateful old goat, thought Ian as he opened the door to Susan's room with his foot.

Like the rest of the TARDIS Susan's room had been plunged into a semi-darkness, and though Ian's eyes had now become accustomed to the gloom, he still moved around the unfamiliar room with care. He found the bed and laid Susan gently upon it.

Looking about the room he saw an antique oil lamp on a table and he lit it with a match from the box in his pocket. The flickering flame of the lamp distorted and magnified the shadows on the wall, but he was grateful for the light it afforded him.

He picked up a patchwork quilt which was slung over a chair and covered Susan with it. The girl's pulse was still racing, he noted, and she was running a temperature.

She needed something to keep her cool, he decided. He left the room and went down the corridor to the nearby rest room. The Doctor had shown Ian and Barbara only recently how to operate the food machine, and Ian thought he must have mis-set the controls when the machine clicked and whirred and registered the fact that it was empty of water. Nevertheless, as with Susan before him, a sachet of water was produced and Ian took it, wryly thinking that perhaps the Doctor's genius at inventing gadgets for all manner of things wasn't as good as he made it out to be. Even in his present situation that thought gave him some strange satisfaction: the Doctor wasn't all that clever after all, in spite of all his rhetoric.

When he returned to Susan's room he stopped dead in his tracks. Susan was wide awake and standing stiffly by her bed. Her right arm was raised and in her hand she pointed a pair of long scissors threateningly at Ian.

Ian took an instinctive step backwards and regarded Susan warily. Her face was white, drawn and stretched, her stylishly cropped dark hair a wild mess; her eyes stared wide open and mad, blazing with terror.

'Susan, what are you doing?' he asked softly, at the same time taking a cautious step towards her.

Susan lunged viciously forward with the scissors, warning him not to come any closer. But when she spoke her voice was stilted and staccato, like a robot's. 'Who – are – you –'

'Susan, it's me, Mr Chesterton,' Ian said, and reached a hand forward. 'Give me the scissors, you don't need them.'

'What – are – you – doing – here –' Again that flat, emotionless tone, belied by the fear in her eyes.

'Susan, give me the scissors,' repeated Ian firmly.

Susan stared madly at him and dived forward, aiming for the schoolteacher's face. Ian retreated, just in time to avoid the sharp points of the scissors.

Susan was about to make another attack when her expression changed and she looked curiously at Ian, seeming to recognise him for the first time. She looked confusedly from his face to the scissors in her hand and then back to his face again.

Ian stood by helplessly as Susan wailed with anguish and frustration and fell back weeping onto her bed. Like a person possessed, the fifteen-year-old schoolgirl began to slash with the scissors at the mattress of her bed. This continued for almost a minute and then she fell back onto the bed, teary-eyed and exhausted, burying her head into her pillow.

By her side the scissors clattered and fell, useless, to the floor.

2

The Seeds of Suspicion

As soon as the Doctor had regained his strength, his first concern had been to check on the health of his granddaughter and, with Barbara's support, he had walked shakily down the passageway which led to her room.

When he discovered his granddaughter weeping on her ripped and torn bed, and Ian standing dumbfounded by her, he seemed to recover his former vitality and sharply ushered the two schoolteachers out of the room, closing the door on them.

Ian and Barbara stood outside for long minutes while the Doctor talked to his granddaughter. They exchanged worried, grim looks. Once again they were being made to feel the outsiders on the Ship, excluded from the alien lives of the Doctor and Susan. The them-and-us mentality, so expertly displayed by the Doctor, did nothing for their peace and security on board the TARDIS.

'What happened in there?' asked Barbara.

Ian showed her the scissors he had picked up off the floor of Susan's room. 'I don't know,' he said. 'Susan seemed to go crazy . . . didn't seem to recognise me . . . and then she attacked me with these scissors.'

Barbara expressed disbelief. Ian continued: 'Don't expect me to explain it, Barbara. She was like a person possessed.'

Barbara felt a tingle of fear run down her spine at

Ian's words. She changed the subject. 'What do you think they're talking about in there?'

Ian shrugged. 'How should I know? No doubt we'll find out when they're good and ready.'

Finally the door opened and the Doctor came out.

'Susan is resting peacefully now,' he said. 'I've given her a mild sedative.' He paused to give the two teachers a withering look, as if to accuse them for Susan's confused state of mind, and which clearly expressed the very low opinion he had of them. 'Now I suggest that we put our heads together and discuss our current predicament.'

He led the way to the rest room and eased himself onto the Chippendale *chaise-longue*, childishly taking up the whole of the seat so that Ian and Barbara were forced to stand. When he spoke it was as though he were addressing a group of slightly dim-witted students, and did not encourage any interruptions. Like so many of the Doctor's 'discussions' this one was no more than an opportunity for him to hold forth before a captive audience.

'Now this is the situation as I see it,' he began. 'We have suffered a massive explosion, the result of which has been that the main drive and power functions of the TARDIS have been massively curtailed. As of yet we have no means of establishing the cause of this explosion or how seriously the rest of the Ship has been affected. Susan has suggested to me that the TARDIS has stalled, and somehow become trapped within the time vortex. That I dispute. All indications on the parts of the control board which are still operational tell me that we are still in flight; and yet the time rotor is motionless suggesting that we have, in fact, materialised. The time rotor is one of the most sensitive instruments on board my Ship and I feel much more inclined to believe that. We have undoubtedly landed.'

'But where?' persisted Barbara. 'Where are we?' The old man's steady logical tone was beginning to infuriate her.

The Doctor shook his head and raised a hand to silence her. 'Tut, tut, all these questions, Miss Wright . . .'

His patronising tone finally proved too much for the former history teacher. 'You just don't know, do you!' she snapped. 'For all your pontificating and high-minded attitude you're as much in the dark as the rest of us. Why don't you admit that you haven't the faintest idea what has happened to us and let us all try and solve this problem together?'

'My dear Miss Wright, I have many more years of experience than you can ever have dreamed of,' retorted the Doctor, furious at having his ability called into question by a mere twentieth-century Earth school-teacher. 'I have studied at the greatest institutions and with the most brilliant minds in the entire universe. If I cannot find the answers to this problem then I doubt very much whether your primitive mind can even dis-cover the questions!'

Barbara darted a look of sheer, undisguised hate at the pompous, arrogant old man. If Ian had not laid a restraining hand on her shoulder there was no telling what she might have done; but the chances are that it would not have done the Doctor's health any good.

Instead she contented herself with glaring at him and then walked smartly out of the rest room in disgust.

Ian was more level-headed than Barbara and, though the Doctor's arrogant and abrasive attitude infuriated him just as much, he thought it wiser to appeal to the Doctor's vanity. The man was insufferable, certainly, but he was unfortunately speaking the truth: he was indeed the only one who could rescue them from their present predicament. It would do well to flatter him for the moment.

'You must surely have some idea where we are, Doctor,' he said gently.

'*Where* isn't as important as *why*, young man,' the old man said, neatly sidestepping the question. 'I have to confess that I am somewhat at a loss in this situation. Something like this has never affected the TARDIS before. But every problem has its solution. There must be an answer, there must be!'

'Perhaps the Fault Locator can tell us?' suggested Ian. He was referring to a large bank of computers in the control room which monitored and regulated every performance of the TARDIS. If any part of the time-machine was damaged in any way, the Fault Locator would point out the area to be repaired.

The Doctor nodded approvingly and led the way out of the rest room, clicking his fingers as he would if he were calling a pet poodle to heel. Ian bit his lip in an effort to control his temper and followed.

When the two men reached the control chamber Barbara was already there, standing stiffly in the shadows by the Doctor's ormolu clock, her arms folded in barely concealed irritation. She looked venomously at the Doctor and then turned sulkily away.

The Doctor ignored her, and turned to Ian. 'You didn't touch the controls, did you?' he asked.

'No,' said Ian. 'Something seemed to happen every

time we tried to approach one of the control panels. Some sort of electrical discharge, I imagine.'

'Did you?' the Doctor asked Barbara. Her stony silence was answer enough.

The Doctor tapped his fingers together. 'I know Susan wouldn't touch the controls without my permission . . .' He shook his head. 'I worry about that girl,' he said, almost talking to himself. 'This temporary lapse of memory is most disturbing . . . it's never happened before. She's always been a very sensitive child; the shock of the explosion must have been much more traumatic than we thought . . .'

Barbara, who had been staring into space, looked over at Ian. 'I was thinking . . .' she began tentatively.

His recent *contretemps* with the schoolteacher already forgotten, the Doctor seized eagerly on her words. 'Yes, what is it? Anything may help.'

Barbara lowered her eyes to avoid the Doctor's stare as she said, 'Well . . . do you think something might have got inside the Ship?'

'Pschaw!' said the Doctor scornfully, responding exactly as Barbara had feared he would. 'My ship is inviolable, sacrosanct! Nothing, physical or mental can penetrate its exterior defences without my express permission.'

Barbara looked up at the old man, and stared him straight in the eyes. 'The doors were open,' she stated flatly.

'Don't be ridiculous!' The Doctor's temper was rising again. 'Susan said that too when I talked to her; but she must have been hallucinating. The doors cannot open unless the controls are operated. The very idea that they can be forced open by an outside power is

37

preposterous!'

Intrigued by Barbara's theory, Ian ignored the Doctor, much to the latter's indignation. 'What do you mean, something might have got into the Ship?' he asked her. 'A man or something?'

Barbara nodded.

'It's not very logical, is it?' chided the Doctor, as though he were berating a rather dull student. 'Really, Miss Wright . . .'

'Or something else . . .' continued Barbara. 'Another intelligence perhaps . . .'

The Doctor snorted scornfully. 'As I said, Miss Wright, it's not very logical, is it?'

'No, it isn't – but does it have to be!' burst out Barbara, angered once again by the Doctor's lofty attitude. 'Perhaps I am overreacting to the situation; perhaps I am letting my imagination run away with me. But at least I am trying to come up with some answers. And anyway, what if it isn't logical? Why don't you admit that things aren't always logical? After all we've been through –'

The Doctor wagged an admonishing finger at Barbara. 'Really, Miss Wright,' he said patronisingly, 'if you can't contribute anything useful to our discussions I suggest you –'

'Well, what do you suggest? You're being so very high and mighty. You're supposed to have all the answers. So *you* tell us what's happening around here. Go on – tell us!'

The Doctor turned away from her. Barbara had touched a raw nerve. 'I have been very patient with you, Miss Wright,' he prevaricated. 'But really, there is no more time for any of your absurd theories.'

Ian attempted to calm the tension which was building up between the Doctor and Barbara. 'It's probably only a mechanical fault,' he said reasonably.

'Exactly!' said the Doctor, pleased that at least one of his two ludicrous human companions was showing a little bit of common sense. 'A mechanical fault, that's what it must be. But what worries me is that it may be the main power unit. If that is the fault it could cause us quite a bit of trouble. If this is the case I shall have to attend to the TARDIS's engines.'

He turned back to Ian, once more ill-manneredly ignoring Barbara. 'Young man, now that Susan is out of action I think that you will have to try and help me with the Fault Locator. It won't take long.'

Ian nodded but added a word of caution. 'All right. But I wouldn't go near the central console if I were you, Doctor. It might give you an electric shock!'

'What? Oh yes, a very wise piece of advice indeed, Chesterton. Now do come along!'

The Doctor crossed over the floor of the control room towards the unit which held the Fault Locator computer. Before he joined him Ian turned back to Barbara who was standing by the door which led into the other parts of the Ship.

'I swear I'm going to throttle him one day,' Barbara said.

Ian smiled. 'You'll have to get in the queue,' he said. 'Barbara –'

'Keep an eye on Susan?'

Ian nodded. 'Don't tell her about anything being on the Ship,' he whispered, sounding almost conspiratorial. 'The less said, the better.'

'Come along, Chesterton!' the Doctor called impatiently from the other end of the control room.

Ian shrugged and went over to join his older companion. Barbara paused for a moment before leaving the room, giving Susan, who had been standing unseen in the doorway, listening, the chance to stride back down the corridor to her room. As she passed through the rest room she quickly picked up the pair of scissors which Ian had relieved her of and placed there earlier. She had heard every word spoken by Ian and Barbara.

Don't tell her about anything being on the Ship. So, reasoned Susan in her confused state of mind, something had indeed come aboard the TARDIS. And what was more, Ian and Barbara knew what it was.

The Fault Locator was, in fact, a series of computers and monitors which lined one entire wall of the TARDIS control room. It was separated from the rest of the chamber by a large transparent screen.

Most of the half-light in the control room found its source here; for some reason the strange power loss which affected most of the TARDIS's instruments did not seem to have influenced the Fault Locator. The only other source of illumination in the room appeared to come from the overhead shaft of light above the time rotor in the centre of the control console.

The Doctor indicated a VDU screen to Ian. 'Now, young man, what you will see on that screen is a series of letters and numbers. Each one represents a particular piece of instrumentation on board my Ship. Should any of those numbers flash that will mean that that piece of equipment is malfunctioning.'

Ian signalled his understanding and the Doctor punched out a program on the Fault Locator's com-

40

puter keyboard. A series of consecutive numbers began to appear before Ian's eyes.

Ian stared at the digital read-out for ten minutes, his face macabrely illuminated by the emerald green glow of the video screen. Finally every single piece of machinery and instrumentation in the TARDIS had been accounted for. He turned to the Doctor who was expectantly awaiting his report.

'Well, Chesterton?' he asked impatiently. 'What does the Fault Locator say? What's wrong with my Ship?'

Ian frowned. 'That's just the trouble, Doctor,' he said. 'According to this nothing at all is wrong with the TARDIS. Every single piece of equipment is functioning perfectly.'

'Preposterous!' mocked the Doctor. 'Our power has been seriously curtailed. According to you and Miss Wright the doors seem to be opening of their own accord. Susan says the Food Machine is malfunctioning. There must be something wrong. Are you sure you've read the instruments correctly?'

'I did exactly what you told me to do, Doctor,' Ian replied peevishly. 'Look for yourself if you don't believe me. I even double-checked the mechanism for opening the doors and for providing food and water. Every single instrument of the TARDIS is in perfect working order – and yet nothing is working. Could there be a malfunction in the Fault Locator itself?'

The Doctor shook his head. 'No no no, that's impossible. The Fault Locator works on a different system and power source altogether; it has to by its very nature.' He frowned and scratched his chin. 'Every single mechanism in the Ship is supposedly functioning

41

perfectly and yet we are suffering this strange power loss. I wonder . . .' The Doctor stroked his chin and looked thoughtfully at Ian.

'Yes, Doctor?' asked Ian in anticipation.

'I think that you and I, young man, should go down to the TARDIS's engine and power rooms,' he said finally. 'The Fault Locator is not registering a malfunction on board my Ship, so it will be necessary for us to examine the Ship's drive mechanisms for ourselves. Are you in agreement?'

Ian frowned, oddly disturbed by the almost eager manner in which the Doctor asked the question. But nevertheless he nodded his head in agreement.

'Where are the power rooms, Doctor?' he asked. 'You've never spoken of them before.'

'Deep down in the very heart of my Ship, Chesterton,' said the Doctor. 'They form the very nerve centre of my machine.'

The Doctor left the area of the Fault Locator and crossed the floor of the control chamber. He opened up one of the roundels on the wall to reveal a small storage unit from out of which he took two small oil lamps, similar to the one in Susan's bedroom. He lit them and passed one to Ian.

'It will be very dark down there,' explained the Doctor. 'These will afford us some light.'

'Oil lamps?' asked Ian quizzically. 'Surely that's a little primitive?'

'We have no way of knowing what manner of force is draining away the power from my Ship,' replied the Doctor. 'But whatever it is I doubt very much that it can effect something as primitive and simple as the combustion of oil.'

Smiling in spite of himself, Ian followed the Doctor through the open doorway and into the interior of the TARDIS.

3

Inside the Machine

The path the Doctor took Ian led him down through long winding narrow corridors, the existence of which he had never before suspected. These passages were even darker than the rest of the Ship, and the light from the oil lamps allowed them to see only a few feet in front of them.

In the darkness, the rhythmic in-out in-out breathing of the life support system seemed even more eerily alive. Ian shuddered, but resisted the urge to share his fears with the Doctor who would only delight in ridiculing his irrational notions.

The Doctor walked down the corridors at a brisk trot, stopping only occasionally to check his way. To Ian it seemed as if the Doctor was trying to lose him in the darkness; for an old man his pace was surprisingly quick and Ian often found himself having to increase his step to catch up with him.

The walls of the corridors were covered with the roundels common to all parts of the TARDIS, and every ten feet or so were interrupted by a closed door. Sometimes they would open one of these doors and enter the corridor beyond it. Ian asked the Doctor where the other doors led to but the Doctor's only response was a muttered suggestion that he mind his own business. Ian wondered whether the Doctor really did know what lay behind all these locked doors, or for that matter exactly where he was going.

'Just how far does the TARDIS go on for, Doctor?' Ian asked after they had been following the same interminable corridor for ten minutes. 'Surely it must have an end somewhere?'

'The interior dimensions in the Ship are merely relative to the exterior universe, Chesterton,' said the Doctor as if that explained everything.

Ian shrugged and continued to follow the old man; if the Doctor didn't want to admit that he didn't have the faintest idea of what he was talking about, then that was his own affair.

The Doctor was, in fact, being unusually silent, as though he were wrestling with some important issue in his mind. Finally despairing of ever getting any intelligent conversation out of him, Ian contented himself with examining in the flickering light of the oil lamp some of the many items and *objets d'art* which lined the walls.

The Doctor, it seemed, was an avid collector of antiques from every period of history; there were delicate Ming vases from China and finely carved baroque chairs from England, as well as weird-looking futuristic items which Ian didn't recognise but supposed came from one of the alien planets the Doctor had visited with his granddaughter. Many were obviously placed there for decoration, but as the two men descended deeper into the TARDIS and the corridors became sparser it was apparent that many others had been left there a long time ago and simply forgotten.

They came to an intersection of four corridors and the Doctor paused, as if he was unsure of which direction to take. While the Doctor deliberated, Ian's attention was drawn to a pile of five dusty paintings which had been dumped unceremoniously on an old threadbare sofa by the wall.

He bent down to examine them more closely in the light from the oil lamp. Four of them were Italian pastoral scenes, pleasant to look at but showing no great talent. But the fifth one made Ian catch his breath.

It was an arresting portrait of a young handsome courtier; in the bottom right-hand corner was signed the name 'Leonardo'.

Ian whistled with appreciation. 'Doctor, do you realise what you've got here?' he asked incredulously. 'A lost Leonardo like this is absolutely priceless – Doctor? Doctor?'

Ian looked all around him. The Doctor was nowhere to be seen. Ian was left alone in the dark threatening confines of the TARDIS interior.

Ian shouted down the corridors after the Doctor. But if the old man was there he didn't hear him; the only reply was the monotonous in-out in-out breathing which in the darkness, and now that Ian was alone, sounded louder than ever.

Trying not to panic, Ian realised that there was no point in trying to go after the Doctor. His chance of finding the old man in the maze of passageways would be impossible; if the TARDIS was indeed as big as he suspected he could be lost there for days. Better, he reasoned, to retrace his steps back to a part of the TARDIS which he recognised and from there find Susan who would surely know her way around the Ship's corridors.

Using as points of reference the antiques he had seen

on his journey down the corridor, Ian began to walk back. But to his horror when he reached one of the doors which opened onto the main corridor that led up to the main area of the TARDIS, and which had been open when they had passed it before, he found that it was locked shut. Vainly he tried to open it but it refused to yield to his touch. In a futile gesture he pounded on the door and called out for help; but the only answer was the mocking breathing of the life support system.

In desperation he looked around for another entrance into the control centre of the Ship. But he knew he had no choice: his only possible route was back down into the depths of the Ship. Resigned, he followed the corridor he had taken with the Doctor.

He seemed to walk for miles; and as he did so it occurred to him that the TARDIS corridors seemed somehow different. It took him a while to realise that doors which had before been open were now firmly closed, and doors which had been locked shut were now open.

He reached the intersection of three corridors and, despite himself, stood and watched in amazement as two of the three doors slammed shut in his face, thereby leaving him no choice but to go through the one door that remained open. And as he passed through a doorway that door too would close soundlessly behind him, thereby cutting off his only means of retreat.

Ian felt the hairs on the back of his neck rise and he tried to shrug off the notion that someone was watching him and mapping out his route for him, as dispassionately as a human scientist would watch a mouse trapped in the maze of some scientific experiment.

Occasionally he would stop at a door which was not

locked and look into the room beyond. But invariably these rooms would be closed off, and the gothic treasures which they housed, together with that infernal in-out in-out breathing and the darkness, did nothing to calm his nerves.

Finally he admitted defeat and almost meekly followed the route which was somehow being chosen for him.

Within minutes the descent of the corridor seemed to level off. Ian found himself in a large, featureless unfurnished anteroom. The in-out in-out breathing was almost deafening down here and, to make matters worse, the light in the room pulsed up and down in brilliance in accordance with the breathing, plunging the room one moment into pitch darkness and then into searing brightness. The entire effect was quite disorientating and Ian had to lean against one wall to maintain his balance.

He tried three of the four doors which led off from the anteroom. They were all securely locked. He was about to try the fourth door when it slowly began to creak open. The lights in the anteroom faded all together, until the only one in it was the ever-widening arc from the opening door.

With no place to run or hide, Ian stepped back in horror as a shadowy threatening figure appeared silhouetted in the doorway.

4

Trapped

'Chesterton, what on Earth are you doing there?'

Ian breathed a sigh of relief, which rapidly turned to embarrassed anger as he recognised the Doctor's voice. Nevertheless he controlled his temper.

'I . . . I got lost,' he said lamely.

The Doctor tut-tutted. 'You should have kept up with me,' he reprimanded; but did Ian detect a glint of malicious amusement in the old man's eyes?

'I did do!' he protested. 'But I stopped for a moment and the next minute you were gone!'

'If you must go wandering off on your own what do you expect?' chastised the Doctor. 'Although goodness knows how you found your way down here.' He imperiously beckoned Ian forward. 'Now, do come along – we haven't got all day you know!'

Ian eyed the Doctor suspiciously; disconcerted by the old man's lack of concern about his plight, but recognising that he had no alternative, he followed him down a winding spiral staircase which he surmised must lead to the very deepest part of the TARDIS.

If he had thought to look he would have noticed that all the doors he had passed which had been locked now miraculously opened by themselves . . .

The in-out in-out breathing which permeated the TARDIS and the pulsating lights which Ian had noticed in the anteroom had their origin in the Ship's power rooms. This was a series of fifteen interconnected rooms containing all the machinery and power sources which operated the TARDIS.

Here, explained the Doctor, were the regulators and engines which powered every function of the TARDIS: its lighting and heat, its life supports, its navigation and memory banks, and, most importantly of all, the drive mechanisms which powered it on its journeys throughout space and time.

Ian noted with wry amusement that, although all these machines were undoubtedly centuries ahead of his own understanding, they still retained, with their elaborate brass fittings and antiquated pistons and levers, all the magical Edwardian splendour of a Heath Robinson mechanism, as though the Doctor had imprinted his own fascination with the Edwardian era onto his machine.

Ian glanced around the room. Apart from the pulsing lights, the area was in darkness. The machines were dusty, and even the normally sterile atmosphere of the TARDIS here was dull and muggy, as though the rooms had never been used or visited in a long long time. Littering the floor were large leatherbound technical manuals, their bindings worn with age.

Every single movable part of every single machine was motionless and silent, but when Ian and the Doctor examined them more closely they found that they were still warm, as though they had been in operation but a few minutes ago.

The Doctor crossed over to the door which, he said mysteriously, led into the 'power stacks' of the TARDIS. He frowned as he turned and twisted the handle.

'What's the matter, Doctor?' Ian asked.

'The door seems to be locked,' said the Doctor. 'Now that's most unusual . . . I wanted to check the power gauges . . .'

'Tell me, Doctor,' said Ian as the old man came back over and bent down to examine a video screen on one of the banks of computers which lined the room, 'what is that infernal noise all around us?'

'Noise?' queried the Doctor.

'That sort of breathing,' explained Ian.

The Doctor snorted superiorly. 'Oh that,' he said. 'Why, it's the life support systems, of course . . . Whatever did you think it was?'

Ian ignored the question and continued: 'And the main controls of the life support system are housed down here?'

'Of course,' said the Doctor, and then realised what Ian was trying to say.

He indicated a large intricately constructed mechanism on the wall which Ian laughingly thought resembled a large pair of bellows.

'And yet the life support mechanism itself, the system which provides us with all our oxygen, Earth-type gravity and heat, and protects us from the time vortex, is not functioning . . .'

'Just like everything else down here,' added Ian. 'Doctor, what exactly is going on? By rights we should have been dead long ago. But even though not one major machine in the TARDIS is functioning, we're still alive!'

The Doctor directed Ian's attention to the video screen he was examining which, like several minor and unimportant instruments on board the Ship, was still operating normally.

'And this indicates that all the power necessary for the smooth running of my Ship is being generated and channelled correctly,' he said, 'and yet not one iota of it is being used to power the mechanisms of my Ship.'

'As if all the power is being drawn off somewhere before it reaches the machines,' reasoned Ian. 'But if that's the case, why is the life support system still operating and keeping us alive?'

'How am I supposed to know, Chesterton!' snapped the Doctor. 'I'm not a miracle worker!'

Ian muttered a half-hearted apology, only vaguely aware that he had touched a raw nerve in the Doctor. The Doctor liked to pretend that he was the absolute master of his Ship; the truth was that he understood very little about its mechanisms and the way it operated.

'So what do we do now, Doctor?' asked Ian, in an attempt to change the subject and assuage the old man's wounded pride.

The Doctor paused for a moment and looked thoughtfully at Ian. Then he pointed to an open door at the far end of the room. 'In there you will find the internal scanner, Chesterton. It is designed to give a general visual overview of all the TARDIS's power rooms. If my machines cannot tell me what is affecting the Ship's power perhaps the eye can. The machine is very simple to operate. I suggest you go in there and report your findings to me.'

Ian nodded. He crossed over to open the door and entered the room, watched closely by the Doctor.

The room was small, about the size of a dentist's waiting room, and featureless apart from the usual

TARDIS wall roundels. In the corner, as the Doctor had said, was a video screen and control panels, housed in an ornate mahogany cabinet, rather like an old-fashioned television set. Following the Doctor's instructions, Ian bent down and switched on the machine.

The screen buzzed into life and began to show a succession of pictures of all of the TARDIS's fifteen different power rooms. Each was in darkness and silent, their machines no longer operating.

Ian studied the pictures one more time and then called out to the Doctor. 'They're exactly like everywhere else, Doctor,' he said. 'Dark and silent –'

He stopped and turned around anxiously when the Doctor did not reply. The door behind him was closed. Panicking, he stood up and tried to open it; it was locked firmly shut.

He banged on the door and called out the Doctor's name but there was no response from the old man. Beads of perspiration appeared on Ian's forehead; ever since a child Ian had had a fear of being trapped in a confined space, and now the four walls of the room seemed to crowd threateningly upon him.

His heart missed a beat as he realised that the air inside the room was rapidly becoming stale and stuffy.

He called out the Doctor's name once more, using up valuable oxygen, and rattled at the door handle. But the door refused to budge. Frantically he looked around for anything with which he could lever the door open, but apart from the internal scanner the room was bare. There did not seem to be any visible locking mechanism on the door, or an electronic circuit which he could trip.

He pressed against the door with all his weight, but it

refused to give. His futile beating on the door became weaker as the life-giving oxygen in the room remorselessly ran out. His heart and lungs pounded painfully in his chest as he struggled to gasp whatever air he could.

Through fogged eyes he looked at the room which began to spin sickeningly around him. Close to unconsciousness, he fell despairingly to his knees.

Click!

Ian raised his head and gulped in gratefully the rush of air which flooded into the room as the door creaked slowly open. Raising himself with difficulty onto his feet, he staggered through the now open door and into the power rooms beyond.

To Ian's surprise the Doctor had not opened the door. Instead he was standing some way off, absorbed in examining a piece of equipment. He started when he saw Ian coming out of the room.

'Doctor,' groaned Ian, 'didn't you hear me?'

'Hear you? What on earth are you talking about, Chesterton?'

'That room back there . . . I was trapped . . . air running out . . .'

The Doctor turned his eyes almost nervously away from the young schoolteacher and continued to examine the piece of equipment. Finally he put it down on a small work bench. 'Well, you're safe now,' he said. 'And since nothing seems to be working down here I see little point in staying around. Shall we join the others?'

Ian regarded the Doctor suspiciously. The old man was behaving very strangely, almost guiltily. Ian knew so little about the Doctor, but one thing he did know was that the old man had a completely alien set of codes and morals to those of him and Barbara.

56

Could it be possible that he had actually deliberately locked Ian in that room, with the express intention of getting him out of the way – permanently? Though he had known the Doctor for such a short measure of time Ian wouldn't have put it past him.

But if the Doctor had locked him in the room, then how had the door become unlocked? Had the Doctor had a sudden change of heart?

'Well, Chesterton?' asked the Doctor irritably. 'I said, shall we join Susan and Miss Wright?'

Ian nodded. 'Fine, Doctor,' he said. 'But this time I think you had better lead the way.'

The Doctor eyed Ian viciously, and then led the way out of the power rooms and into the corridors outside. All the doors which had before been securely closed were now open again.

As the Doctor and Ian left the power rooms, all the machines which had been silent and motionless during their visit, suddenly chattered into life again . . .

'Your companion, Miss Wright,' began the Doctor, as he and Ian walked up the corridor.

'Barbara,' corrected Ian.

'Yes, quite,' continued the Doctor. 'Your companion, Miss Wright, suggested that the problem might lie not in the TARDIS itself but in some sort of outside entity –'

'Which you said was ridiculous,' Ian reminded him pointedly.

The Doctor caught the implied criticism in Ian's voice but chose to ignore it. 'And which I still maintain is impossible. But it is still feasible that we are in the grip of some powerful force which exists outside the

Ship.'

   'So? What do you suggest we do?'

   'Simplicity itself, Chesterton! We see what's outside the Ship!'

5

'Like a Person Possessed'

When Barbara had returned to Susan's room her former pupil seemed to be sleeping peacefully. A good sleep was exactly what the girl needed, reflected Barbara. Susan had always seemed more sensitive than her other pupils; recent events had obviously shaken her up quite a lot. Her attempted attack on Ian was merely a symptom of her inner turmoil and frustration.

Barbara sat at her bedside, checking her pulse from time to time and ensuring that everything was all right with her charge. On a table the oil lamp which Ian had lit still cast eerie shadows on the wall.

The rhythmic in-out in-out sound of the Ship's life support system which seemed to have replaced the normally ubiquitous humming of the TARDIS's machinery, was vaguely soporific and Barbara found herself beginning to nod off to sleep.

A sudden noise awoke her with a start.

Barbara was alert in an instant, her nerves tingling. By her side Susan had sat bolt upright in bed, her hands still hidden underneath the covers. Barbara smiled with more than a little relief, chiding herself for her nervousness.

'How are you feeling now?' she asked.

Susan looked at her strangely. Perhaps she was still slightly concussed, thought Barbara.

'I'm fine,' the schoolgirl said slowly. 'Why shouldn't

I be?'

'Susan, you do remember who I am, don't you?'
Barbara asked. Susan's voice sounded oddly clipped;
for an awful moment it reminded Barbara of the
staccato emotionless tones of the Dalek creatures they
had encountered on the planet Skaro. She was suddenly
very worried.

'Of course I remember who you are,' the girl continued in the same flat monotone. 'You're Barbara.'

Barbara's brow furrowed with concern as she
registered Susan's unfamiliar use of her first name. Up
till now Susan had always referred to her, in her
presence at least, as Miss Wright, retaining some of the
teacher-pupil respect which had been encouraged at
Coal Hill. Her sudden use of the name Barbara un-
nerved the schoolteacher.

Shrugging off her vague suspicions, Barbara felt
Susan's forehead. Her temperature was still un-
commonly high. She crossed over to the dressing table
where, by the oil lamp, Ian had placed a bowl of water.
She dipped her large handkerchief into it, squeezed it of
any excess moisture and then returned to Susan. 'Put
this on your forehead, Susan,' she said. 'It'll keep you
cool.'

'Why?' asked the girl. 'There's nothing wrong with
me. There's no need to cosset me like I was Tiny Tim or
something.'

'Who?' Barbara asked sharply.

'Tiny Tim,' repeated Susan. 'He was the young
cripple in Charles Dickens' *Christmas Carol*.'

'I didn't think you knew any Dickens,' Barbara said
slowly. She suddenly remembered something Mr
Foster the English teacher had once said to her: that girl

Foreman, brilliant in some respects – she can recite quite huge hunks of Shakespeare as if she really knew him. But she's never even read a word of Dickens!

Susan flushed and Barbara imagined that she had somehow upset the girl.

'I – I must have heard Grandfather talking about him sometime . . . He's very well read, you know . . .'

Barbara looked at Susan suspiciously. The abrupt changes of mood, the violence, this piece of knowledge . . . was this really Susan she was talking to, or . . . She shuddered at the thought of the alternative.

Like a person possessed, Ian had said. Barbara tried to humour her. 'Of course there's nothing wrong with you, Susan,' she said. 'You just need a rest, that's all.'

Susan seemed to acquiesce and sank back down onto her pillows. Suddenly she sat back up again, and clutched Barbara's arm. 'Where's Grandfather?' Her voice had suddenly changed: no longer was it emotionless and cold; there was no mistaking the concern in it.

Barbara loosed herself from Susan's grip, and replied. 'He's checking the controls with Ian – Mr Chesterton.'

Susan's face seemed to relax and then she said, 'Why did you ask me if I knew who you were?'

'It's just that before you seemed to . . .' Barbara felt embarrassed, unsure of how to answer the girl's question. How do you tell someone that you suspect they're losing their grip on reality?

Susan continued to stare at her in an odd way. Underneath the covers Barbara was aware of Susan's hands fumbling with something.

Barbara held out her hand. 'Susan, why don't you give me the scissors?' she said with gentle firmness.

Susan drew her hand out from under the pillow and pointed the instrument threateningly at Barbara.

'Susan, give them to me!' Barbara commanded in her best schoolmarm voice, the voice which used to strike terror into the hearts of class 1C.

The girl seemed to hesitate but still pointed the scissors at Barbara. Her hand was trembling. In this nervous state Barbara realised she could be capable of anything. The schoolteacher tried a different tack. 'Susan, what is all this about?' she asked softly and reasonably.

'You said there had been a power failure,' she began.

Barbara corrected her. 'No, I didn't. I said that's what Ian thinks.'

'I don't believe you,' Susan continued. 'You lied to me.'

'Lied to you? What are you talking about, Susan?'

'I overheard you and Mr Chesterton. You said there was something in the Ship, something you didn't want me to know about . . .'

Realisation suddenly dawned for Barbara. 'I see – you just overheard a few words and you –'

'No,' interrupted Susan. 'You lied to me. You cannot be trusted.'

'We wouldn't do a thing to hurt you, Susan,' insisted Barbara. 'Surely you know that by now?'

'No. You're frightened of us, Grandfather and me. You're different from us. How can we know what you're thinking, what you think of us?'

'Susan, don't you see it's the same for all of us? You and your grandfather are as alien to us as we are to you. Maybe there are times when we don't know where we stand with you; yes, maybe there are times when we are frightened of you, uneasy and uncertain. I know we're all unwilling fellow travellers, and the only thing Ian and I really want to do is go home. But, Susan, we're all in this together whether we like it or not and we have to learn to trust each other. Besides, why should we hurt you and your grandfather? Without the Doctor how can we ever hope to return to Earth in our own time? We might not understand you all the time, but we need you. Can't you see that? Why should we ever try and hurt you?'

Susan lowered the scissors slightly as she considered Barbara's words. Taking advantage of her hesitation, Barbara darted forward, and wrenched the scissors from Susan's hand.

For a few brief moments Susan struggled, hitting at Barbara with her fists in frustration. Then she burst into tears, falling into Barbara's welcoming arms.

Sitting on the edge of the bed Barbara comforted Susan, holding her in her arms and rocking her back and forth like a little child. After a few minutes Susan's weeping subsided and she raised her tear-stained face to look at Barbara. There was no need for words; Barbara recognised the contrition in Susan's eyes; but she also saw the terror.

'Barbara, what's happening to us?' Susan sobbed. Susan's use of her first name no longer upset Barbara.

'I really don't know, Susan. We're . . . we're all just a little upset, that's all. But don't worry. Your grandfather will find out what's wrong with the TARDIS soon, and then we'll be on our way.'

Susan nodded, and then looked around her room. On the bedside table the oil lamp was flickering low. 'I've never noticed the shadows before,' Susan said. 'It's usually so bright . . . But in these shadows there could be anything . . . there are parts of the TARDIS which even I haven't explored properly yet . . .'

'Don't be silly, Susan,' Barbara chastised gently. 'You're tired and you're letting your imagination run away with you. There's nothing to be afraid of in the dark.'

'It's so silent in the Ship,' continued Susan. 'Apart from the breathing.'

'The breathing?'

'Listen – the life support system. It's just like someone breathing, isn't it?' she said darkly.

Barbara hushed her. 'We're imagining things, we must be.' Susan looked at her oddly, almost challenging her to provide an explanation. 'Let's be logical about it, Susan,' continued Barbara. 'I mean, how could anything get into the Ship anyway?'

'The doors were open,' Susan reminded her. 'In spite of what Grandfather says, they were open.'

'But where could it hide?'

'In one of us.'

Barbara shivered as Susan expressed her unvoiced fear. They had all been behaving oddly; could it be that some unknown alien intelligence had penetrated the TARDIS's defences and possessed one of them?

Once again she remembered Ian's words: *like a person possessed*.

'Don't be silly, Susan,' she said weakly. 'We must stop talking like this. Can you imagine what the Doctor and Ian would say if they heard us talking like this? They'd laugh at us. There must be a rational explanation.'

'But supposing there isn't a fault . . .' wondered

Susan.

'You must be clairvoyant!'

Barbara and Susan turned nervously round to see the figure in the open doorway who had come upon them silently. Each of them breathed a sigh of relief when they saw that it was Ian.

'What do you mean?' asked Susan.

'We've just checked everything and according to the Fault Locator the TARDIS is functioning perfectly,' he explained and then looked at Susan. 'How are you feeling now?'

'I'm all right . . . What's my grandfather doing?'

'That's what I came to tell you both. As there's nothing wrong with the TARDIS he's decided that the only fault must lie outside the Ship. He's going to turn on the scanner.'

Susan's face blanched in terror and she leapt out of bed. 'No! He mustn't! He mustn't!' she screamed and ran out of the room.

6

The End of Time

Susan burst into the control room where the Doctor was
about to move to the central control console to operate
the scanner.

'Don't touch it!' she cried.

The Doctor stopped and looked at his granddaughter
curiously. 'Are you all right, child?' he asked.

'Yes, Grandfather,' she replied and indicated the
control console. 'I tried to touch it before and it was like
being hit . . .'

'Hit? Hit where?'

'The back of my neck hurts,' she explained.

The Doctor nodded sagely. 'Rather like mine, in
fact . . .'

Ian and Barbara had entered the control room to hear
the final part of this conversation. 'Funny – it didn't
affect me and Barbara like that,' said Ian.

The Doctor looked at him strangely.

'No, it didn't, did it?' His voice was full of suspicion.
He considered the two schoolteachers warily and then
beckoned Susan over to his side.

Susan considered her grandfather's words and then
regarded Ian and Barbara through narrowed, suspicious eyes. 'Yes . . . Grandfather's right. Nothing did
happen to you, did it . . ?'

'What are you implying, Susan?' asked Barbara
sternly. 'Surely we've just gone through all this?'

The girl didn't reply. Sensing Barbara's unease, Ian put a reassuring arm around her shoulders.

'I must discover what is outside the Ship,' the Doctor determined and, ignoring Susan's warning, he approached that part of the console which contained the scanner controls. Gingerly he operated a small lever, and jumped back, as though expecting a shock of some kind. Nothing happened.

He looked back at Ian. 'Well, I didn't get a shock this time, did I?' he said meaningfully.

'What are you trying to say, Doctor?' asked Ian but before the old man could reply Susan turned their attention to the scanner screen set high in the wall.

The scanner lit up, casting an eerie light around the control room, and an image began to resolve itself on the screen.

The picture was one of a pleasant wooded landscape of oak and birch trees. Beyond them gently rolling hills rose up to a brilliantly blue sky, flecked with wisps of snowy white clouds. Over the audio circuits they could hear the sound of birdsong.

So convincing was the image that Ian and Barbara could almost taste the country freshness in the normally antiseptically clean air of the TARDIS.

'That's England!' Barbara said delightedly, and pointed to the hills in the distance. 'Look, those are the Malvern Hills! I used to spend my summers there as a child!'

'Well, what are we waiting for?' asked Ian, his disagreement with the Doctor suddenly completely forgotten. 'Open the doors and let's see for ourselves! I don't know what's been going on, Doctor, but it looks as though you've brought us home!'

The Doctor considered Ian and Barbara's eager faces and then turned back to the scanner. The school-teachers frowned as they sensed his puzzlement.

'What's wrong, Doctor?' Barbara asked, and felt her heart sink.

'This is all very curious,' the Doctor muttered and pointed to the picture on the scanner. 'That can't be what's outside the Ship.'

'What do you mean?' asked Ian.

'Use the intelligence you were born with, Chesterton!' he said irascibly. 'Look at the clouds, the trees. Not one of them is moving – it's merely a photograph!'

As the Doctor spoke those words the doors to the TARDIS suddenly opened and the control room was filled with a searing white light.

'Close the doors!' commanded the Doctor as he covered his eyes from the glare.

Ian moved towards the light but as he did so, the double doors closed of their own accord.

'You see,' said Barbara to the Doctor. 'We were telling the truth before. They did open by themselves. You saw us: neither of us touched the controls!'

'Look!' said Susan and pointed up at the scanner. 'There's another picture now!'

The picture of the Malvern Hills had vanished and had been replaced by one of an alien jungle, full of enormous and weird barbed plants. In the background impossibly huge mountains towered into a savagely orange sky; the cries of wild and ferocious beasts echoed around the control room.

'Where's that?' asked Barbara.

'The planet Quinnius in the fourth galaxy,' replied the Doctor.

'Yes, it's where Grandfather and I nearly lost the TARDIS four of five journeys ago,' offered Susan. 'But that's not what's outside either . . .'

'Can you explain it, Doctor?' asked Ian.

The Doctor crossed the floor of the control room and settled himself in his Louis XIV chair. 'Did I ever tell you that my Ship has a memory bank, hmm?' he asked.

'It records all our journeys,' added Susan helpfully.

'No, you didn't, Doctor,' said Ian.

'Are you absolutely sure, Chesterton? I thought I did . . .'

Before Ian had time to reply Barbara pointed to the scanner. Yet another picture had formed.

This one was of an unfamiliar planet set in the vast darkness of space. As though the scanner was zooming out, the image was quickly replaced by a picture of the same planet, this time much smaller and surrounded by other planets.

This in turn vanished and a picture of a spiral galaxy of countless thousands of stars appeared in its place. Then the screen was filled with a blinding flash of light, before it went blank altogether, plunging the control room once more into shadow.

During this sequence the exit doors had remained firmly closed.

Then after a pause the image of the Malvern Hills reappeared and the sequence began again. The Doctor turned off the scanner.

'Well, what was all that about?' asked Ian, not really expecting an answer from anyone.

The Doctor trained two steely eyes on the figure of the schoolmaster. 'Don't you know?' he asked accusingly. 'I thought you might be able to tell me.'

Ian shook his head. 'Why me?'

The Doctor allowed himself a self-congratulatory chuckle. 'You won't confuse me, you know, no matter how hard you try.'

Ian was beginning to get annoyed. 'Just what exactly are you getting at, Doctor?' he demanded to know.

The Doctor snorted contemptuously and turned away from Ian. He put a protective arm around his granddaughter.

Barbara crossed over to the Doctor and Susan. 'Look, why don't we try and open the doors and see for ourselves?' she said.

The Doctor dismissed her suggestion. 'What is inside my Ship, madam, is more important at the moment!'

'*Inside?*'

'But you've only just told us that the only people inside are ourselves,' protested Ian. 'You said that nothing could get inside the Ship.'

'Precisely!' said the Doctor. 'Nothing can penetrate my Ship, and all the controls are functioning perfectly. Ergo the fault must lie with one of us!'

'Just what are you trying to say, Doctor?' asked Ian warily.

The Doctor pointed a long accusing finger at the two schoolteachers. 'You two are the cause of this disaster! You sabotaged my Ship!'

Barbara tensed and held Ian's arm. 'No, Doctor, you know that's not true . . .' she said.

'You knocked me and Susan unconscious!'

'Don't be ridiculous!' cried Barbara, rising to the defensive. 'We were all knocked out!'

'Grandfather, she is right,' said Susan slowly. 'When I came to, Mr Chesterton was still unconscious.'

71

The Doctor dismissed Susan's comment curtly. 'A charade! They attacked us!'

'Absolute nonsense!' protested Ian.

'And while we were lying helpless on the floor you tampered with the controls!'

'You looked at everything yourself and you couldn't find anything wrong with them!' Ian reminded him, exasperated at the old man's sheer obstinacy. 'You and I checked every single piece of equipment on board the Ship.'

The Doctor seemed taken aback for a moment but he refused to listen to Ian's reasoning. 'No, sir, *we* did not check everything. I programmed the Fault Locator – *you* checked everything!'

Barbara tried to reason with the Doctor. 'But why would we interfere with the controls? What possible reason could we have?'

The answer was obvious to the Doctor. 'Blackmail! You intend to try and force me to return you to England!'

'Oh, don't be so stupid!' said Barbara.

'I am convinced of it,' said the Doctor. 'You both forced your way on board my Ship, intruded upon the lives of my granddaughter and myself; but you were never prepared to accept the consequences of your actions. So now you intend to hold Susan and me prisoner until we agree to take you back to the twentieth-century.'

Barbara was usually slow to anger but this time the Doctor had gone much too far. She shrugged Ian off as he tried to restrain her and she marched up to the Doctor.

'How *dare* you!' she exploded furiously. 'Do you

72

realise, you stupid old man, that you'd have died in the Cave of Skulls if Ian and I hadn't helped you to escape!'

The Doctor pooh-poohed the notion; he had no wish to be reminded of any debt he might hold to these two humans. But Barbara had not finished.

'And what about all we went through on Skaro against the Daleks? Not just for us but for you and Susan too – and all because you tricked us into going down to the Dalek City in the first place!

'*Accuse* us! You ought to go down on your hands and knees and thank us!' She shook her head in despair. 'But oh no, gratitude is the last thing you'll ever have. You think you're so superior, so much greater than everyone else, but when are you ever going to realise that other people are worth just as much as you? We might not be as intelligent as you, we might not have experienced as much but we have feelings. Do you know what they are? It's a concern for your fellow creatures, a belief that no matter what our differences may be we're all in this mess together and we'd better help each other out. We're not just some laboratory animals for you to study, or inferior creatures for you to make use of . . . But oh no, humility is the last thing you'll ever have – or any sort of common sense!'

The Doctor seemed visibly shaken by Barbara's fierce tirade and for once seemed at a loss for words. Barbara stormed off for the living quarters and Ian followed her. As she passed the Doctor's ormolu clock she stopped. A terrified scream burst from her lips and she turned her face away.

The framework of the Doctor's ormolu clock had remained unchanged and as beautifully ornate as ever. But the face itself on which the hours and minutes were displayed was now distorted, almost unreadable, a mass of molten metal, which strangely radiated no heat. Even the Doctor caught his breath in shock as he wondered at the enormity of whatever power could have caused this.

Fearing what they might find, Ian, Barbara and Susan looked down at their wristwatches in grim expectation.

The faces of these too had melted away; it was as though time had stopped for them.

Susan gave an involuntary shudder. 'We're somewhere where time doesn't exist,' she said, 'where nothing exists except us . . .'

'Oh, don't be stupid, Susan!'

Hysterically Barbara tore the watch off her own wrist and flung it across the control room, where the glass shattered into a hundred tiny pieces. Sobbing, she threw herself down into a chair. Susan went instantly to her side to comfort her.

'You can't blame us for this, Doctor,' said Ian evenly and then turned around. The Doctor had disappeared. 'Where is he now for heaven's sake?' he asked irritably.

As if on cue the Doctor entered the room from the passageway which led to the living quarters. He had a beaming smile on his face and in his hands he carried a tray upon which were four plastic cups.

'I've decided we're all somewhat overwrought,' he said genially as he handed out the cups. 'We all need more time to think instead of throwing insults at each other.'

Ian looked at the old man, amazed at his sudden apparent *volte-face*. 'I wish I could understand you, Doctor,' he said, shaking his head. 'One minute you're abusing us and the next you're acting like the perfect butler.'

'We must all calm down and look at the situation logically, my dear boy,' the Doctor said pleasantly. He shot Ian a crafty look which the schoolteacher did not seem to notice.

Ian eyed the liquid in his cup uncertainly and sniffed it: its smell reminded him of apricots and honey. 'What is this?' he asked warily.

'Merely a little nightcap,' answered the Doctor cheerily. 'Something to help us relax and sleep. In the morning things may look a lot clearer.'

'That is, if it is night now,' pointed out Ian and gestured over to the melted clockface. 'We've no longer any way of telling.'

Over in the corner Barbara had calmed down a little, encouraged by Susan. She stood up determinedly and drained her cup. 'Well, whatever time it is, I'm going to bed,' she said, secretly hoping that in sleep she might find some release from the nightmare into which they had all been thrown.

She walked over to the door. Before she left Ian drew her aside. 'Keep your door locked – just in case,' he whispered.

Barbara was about to ask him what he was talking about when he nodded over to the Doctor. On their way from Susan's room back to the control chamber Ian had told her what had happened in the power rooms. He had no way of telling whether the Doctor had indeed tried to kill him. But after that experience Ian wasn't prepared to trust the old man as far as he could throw him.

Over at the other end of the control room the Doctor glared at them suspiciously, and strained to overhear their conversation. Barbara glared back at him and then, saying goodnight to Ian and Susan, she made her way to the sleeping quarters.

Susan approached the Doctor. 'Make it up with her, Grandfather – please,' she said softly.

The Doctor looked down at his granddaughter and snorted indignantly. There was no way he was going to make amends with Barbara; to do so would be to admit some weakness and culpability on his part – and that the Doctor would never allow himself to do. Indeed, it would be tantamount to admitting he was wrong – and the Doctor stubbornly believed that he was never wrong about anything.

Susan shrugged her shoulders in defeat and followed Barbara out of the room.

When the girls had gone, Ian turned back to the Doctor, who was now relaxing in a chair. He seemed purposely to ignore Ian's continued presence in the room.

'Doctor, some very strange things are happening here,' Ian began. 'I feel we are in a very dangerous situation.'

The Doctor raised an eyebrow. 'Oh, do you now?' he asked haughtily.

'Yes, I do,' replied Ian, his tone hardening slightly in automatic response to the Doctor's supercilious manner. 'I think it's time to forget whatever personal quarrels we may have with each other.'

'Really?'

For the sake of us all, stop being so damn superior and acting like a spoilt brat! thought Ian. 'I think you should go and apologise to Barbara,' he said sternly.

'Oh, should I, young man?' the Doctor said.

'Chesterton, the tone you take with me seems to suggest that you consider me as one of your pupils at that preposterous school of yours –'

'That's not fair,' Ian interrupted him.

The Doctor stood up and drew himself up to his full height.

'Young man, I'm afraid we have no time for codes and manners,' he declared loftily, treating Ian exactly as many of his former colleagues would treat a dim-witted pupil. 'I don't underestimate the dangers – if they do indeed exist. But I must have time to think! I have found that rash action is worse than no action at all.'

'I don't see anything rash in apologising to Barbara,' said Ian, and sipped at his drink.

The Doctor merely laughed off-handedly.

'Frankly, Doctor, I find it very difficult to understand you or even to keep pace with you at times,' Ian admitted.

The Doctor's eyes sparkled with conceit. 'You mean to keep one jump ahead of me, Chesterton, and that you will never do. You need my knowledge and my ability to apply that knowledge; and then you need my experience to gain the fullest results.'

'Results?' said Ian, realising how little he knew the old man and remembering the incident in the power rooms. 'Results for good – or for evil?'

'One man's law is another man's crime,' replied the Doctor enigmatically. 'Sleep on it, Chesterton, sleep on it.'

Ian looked curiously at the old man and then drained his cup. He was already feeling very sleepy. Perhaps the Doctor was right after all: perhaps in the morning things would indeed seem clearer. But he would still lock his door – just in case.

The Doctor watched him go and allowed himself a self-satisfied smirk. He chuckled; he really was immensely superior to everyone else on board the Ship, he thought.

On the floor by his side his cup of beverage was left untouched. He was the only one who had not drunk it . . .

'Who's there?' asked Barbara nervously as she heard a faint tapping at her door.

'It's only me – Susan,' was the reply. 'Can I come in?'

Barbara sighed with relief, thankful for any company, and got up out of bed to unlock the door. Susan was standing there in her nightgown.

Susan looked down, trying hard to avoid Barbara's eyes. 'I just came to say I'm sorry for what Grandfather said to you . . .'

Barbara smiled weakly. 'It's all right, Susan,' she lied. 'It's not your fault.'

'I know . . . but you must try and understand him. He's an old man; he's very set in his ways . . . Whatever you might think of him right now he is a good man – and a very kind one too, so kind and generous you wouldn't believe. He's looked after me so well . . .'

'He has a strange way of showing his kindness, Susan,' said Barbara. There was no resentment in the statement; Barbara was merely pointing out a fact.

'Maybe so,' agreed Susan. 'But you don't know the terrible sort of life he's had. He's never had any reason to trust strangers before when even old friends have turned against him in the past; it's so difficult for him to start now . . . But you and Ian are both good people;

please, try and forgive him.'

'Strangers? Is that still all we are to you, Susan – after all we've gone through?' asked Barbara.

Susan seemed embarrassed. 'No, you know that isn't true . . . but Grandfather . . . please be patient with him . . .'

Barbara was silent for a moment, wondering whether to pursue the matter further tonight.

'Try and get some sleep, Susan,' she advised. 'In the morning it will all seem different.'

'Yes, maybe you're right,' the girl said and yawned. 'I'm feeling quite sleepy already.'

'Can you find your way back to your room in the dark?'

Susan nodded. 'Yes; I know the TARDIS as well as you'd know your own house – it's my home.'

With that she wished Barbara goodnight and went off down the corridor to her bedroom.

Barbara closed and locked the door, realising once again how little she knew of the Doctor and Susan's past. Susan's vague references to it just then troubled her. Why indeed should Susan and the Doctor trust her and Ian? And why, for that matter, should they trust the Doctor and Susan? Despite superficial similarities, she reminded herself once again that they belonged to two entirely different species. Apart from being trapped together in the Ship they had nothing whatsoever in common with each other.

Banishing such doubts from her mind she returned to her bed. She was already feeling very, very sleepy . . .

The Doctor sat in his chair for over an hour, muttering quietly to himself and carefully going over recent events in his head. The drug he had administered to his three companions would give him ample time to think and come up with a way out of this dilemma; and, more importantly, it would keep Ian and Barbara safely out of the way.

The doors had opened, letting in a brilliant white light. Appearances suggested that the doors had opened during flight. Those of the TARDIS's controls which still seemed to be functioning normally certainly appeared to support this supposition. But if that was so why hadn't they been immediately sucked out into the raging time vortex through which they were travelling? And if they were indeed still travelling, why was the central time rotor, which normally rose and fell during flight, motionless?

Therefore, logic decreed that the TARDIS had landed. *But things aren't always very logical, are they?* Barbara had said. The Doctor, whose entire life had been ruled by the application of cold, hard logic and emotionless scientific observation wondered whether the schoolteacher's disturbing proposition was, in fact, a valid one.

But for the moment, he decided, it would be best to follow the path of logical deduction and reasoning, the path he could follow best.

So – the TARDIS had landed somewhere. But where? The multiple images on the scanner did nothing to help; the last one, the one of the exploding star system, was in fact distinctly disquieting.

For a moment the Doctor allowed himself the indulgence of thinking that the sequence of images might be some sort of coded message. But a message from whom? No sooner had the idea crossed his mind than he dismissed it. It was a preposterous notion: nothing could so interfere with the TARDIS without his knowledge and permission.

The Doctor finally eased himself out of his chair. There was only one way to find out where they were. He would not bring himself to admit that it was what Barbara had suggested all along. He would open the doors and venture out of the Ship!

In his bed, Ian tossed and turned, unable to get to sleep. Even the Doctor's drugged drink was having no effect on him. Just as he was about to drop off, the concealed lighting in his room would suddenly flash and rise to a painful brilliance, shocking him out of his drowsiness. Then the lights would fade until his room was as dark and gloomy as the rest of the Ship.

This continued for almost an hour before Ian decided he had had enough. Dragging himself out of bed, he put on a dressing gown and staggered over to the door which he had locked before retiring. Frowning, he noticed that it was now unlocked.

Warily, he opened the door and looked down the corridor. Seeing that no one was out there waiting for him in the shadows, he staggered off to the control room.

Back in his bedroom the lights slowly dimmed and then went out altogether.

7

The Haunting

Back in her room Barbara was experiencing the same difficulties as Ian in getting to sleep. Although Barbara was not aware that she had been drugged, it was as if the pulsing lights which kept her awake were fighting a furious battle with the effects of the Doctor's sleeping drug, intent on keeping her awake.

Finally she resolved to give up the struggle to fall asleep, and got up out of bed. She decided to go down to the rest room and pick up a book to read from the Doctor's wide-ranging library. If she was lucky she would find something by Trollope; if anything could put her to sleep that would.

Slipping into her dressing gown she opened her bedroom door. Although the strange pulsating lights, presumably another malfunction of the TARDIS, had kept her awake, the Doctor's drug was still having a potent effect upon her. If she hadn't been so groggy she would have realised, as Ian had done, that her door had been mysteriously unlocked.

She looked up and down the darkened corridor, trying to remember the way to the rest room; it was so difficult to establish any sense of direction in this gloom. Which way, which way?

Still she could hear the in-out in-out breathing of the TARDIS life support system. Crazily she thought she could hear it changing its rhythm and tone, almost as if

8

it was calling out her name: *Bar-bar-a . . . Bar-bar-a . . .*

She shivered, and then silently scolded herself for behaving like a silly schoolgirl. This was the TARDIS, she reminded herself, a precision-built machine; it was not a Gothic mansion from the latest Hammer horror film.

Nevertheless she walked smartly off in the direction away from the imaginary 'voice' – and, in her super-stition-derived ignorance, also away from the rest room.

Barbara first suspected she was lost when she became aware that the corridor in which she was walking seemed to be sloping downwards – and wasn't the rest room on a slightly higher level than the sleeping quarters? She stopped and looked about her in the half-light.

She had come to a dead end. Behind her wound the corridor she had travelled down; to her sides were two roundelled walls, in one of which there was a door. Deciding that she couldn't get any more lost than she was already she hesitated for a second, and then opened the door.

The door opened out onto a vast laboratory, almost the size of a school assembly hall. Lines of long wooden benches were covered with the most amazing variety of scientific tools Barbara had ever seen in her life. Every-thing from old Chinese abacuses to futuristic items of equipment, the purposes of which Barbara couldn't even guess, seemed to be here.

One entire wall was lined with computers, all of which should have been chattering busily away to each other, but which, like everything else in the TARDIS, were now deathly silent. Another wall was covered with complicated charts and diagrams.

Barbara gave a silent whistle of appreciation; even she, as unscientific as they came, couldn't help but be in awe of the size and comprehensiveness of the Doctor's laboratory.

She gave herself a little pat on the back when she saw the huge shelves on the far wall, packed to overflowing with files, papers and books. She might not have found the rest room, but surely here she would find something to take her mind off her current situation?

But when she reached the bookcase she was sorely disappointed. Book after book was merely another dry scientific treatise. Barbara looked despairingly at what to her was merely mumbo-jumbo, much of it written in strange languages and multisyllabic words she didn't know, or unearthly scripts she couldn't decipher. Sighing, she replaced a book and turned to go.

It was then that she noticed the door which, hidden in the shadows cast from the bookcase, she hadn't seen before. It seemed to be made of some heavy metal and was opened by a rotating circular handle. Curiosity got the better of the schoolteacher and she reached out to open it.

And then her heart missed a beat as a short sharp noise echoed throughout the laboratory. Turning around fearfully, she whispered, 'Who's there?'

No reply.

Barbara looked around and then breathed a sigh of relief as she saw the book on the floor. Obviously she had not replaced all the books carefully enough, and one had dropped to the floor.

Smiling, and chiding herself for her jumpiness, Barbara bent down to pick up the book. But then another book fell off the shelf. And then another. And another. And another – until every single book on the shelf was seemingly throwing itself through the air at Barbara.

Box files fell off the shelves and sprang open, sending their contents swirling and scattering in all directions, as though caught up in some eerie, intangible wind.

Barbara looked on in terror as a whole rack of test tubes swept off a nearby workbench and fell to the floor, smashing into a thousand pieces, their contents giving off noxious fumes.

Other vials and glass tubes rattled madly away in their containers. By her side a chair upended itself and crashed to the floor. Charts fell off the walls, and the floor began to shudder sickeningly beneath her.

'Who's there?' she cried. 'Why don't you just leave me alone!'

But still the nightmarish visitation continued.

Finally Barbara snapped and, terrified, ran out of the room – straight into Susan.

Barbara sobbed with relief when she saw her.

'What is it?' the girl asked.

'In there,' said Barbara, nodding back towards the laboratory. 'There's something in there, throwing about all the books, equipment, everything . . .'

Susan looked warily into the room. The devastation was apparent but nothing was moving there now. 'It's quiet now,' she said, and then asked suspiciously: 'But what were you doing in Grandfather's laboratory?'

'I wanted to get a book,' explained Barbara, gasping for breath. 'But I couldn't find one; so I decided to explore the other rooms in the lab.'

'Other rooms?' asked Susan urgently. 'What other

rooms?'

'Why, the one behind that door,' Barbara said and pointed to the heavy door in the shadows of the bookcase.

Even in the gloom, Barbara could see Susan's face turn chalky white. 'That door . . . do you know what's behind that door?' she asked. Barbara shook her head, and Susan continued. 'Some of Grandfather's experiments require vast amounts of power and radiation – the isotopes are stored behind that lead-screened door. If you'd've gone in there without a protective suit you wouldn't have survived for more than thirty seconds . . .'

'And I was about to open that door,' said Barbara slowly, 'when the attack happened.' She shook her head. 'I don't know what it was, but whatever it was it just saved my life . . .'

'You mean, you really do think that some sort of intelligence has come aboard the TARDIS?'

'Yes, Susan,' said Barbara. 'Don't you feel it too, that feeling that we're being watched all the time?'

Susan shivered. 'Don't let's talk about things like that now,' she urged. 'Let's get back to Grandfather and Ian.'

In the control chamber the Doctor switched on the scanner screen and played back the sequence of images which, like everything else displayed on the screen, had been automatically recorded in the TARDIS's memory banks. Once again the familiar pattern of the Malvern Hills, the planet Quinnius, and the exploding star system was being repeated. This time, however, the exit doors did not open.

He searched his mind, looking for an explanation, but found he could not make head or tail of it. Defeated, he shook his head and deactivated the scanner.

He wandered around the central console to another of its six control panels, the one which included the mechanism which would open the TARDIS's great double doors onto the outside world. For a moment he considered the wisdom of the action he was going to take. Then, flexing his fingers, he lowered one ringed and bony hand down to open the doors.

Before he could reach and operate the control he felt two strong hands close tightly around his neck, dragging him back, attempting to throttle him. In desperation the Doctor struggled to shrug off the attack and then managed to turn around to confront his unknown assailant.

8

Accusations

It was Ian. Wild-eyed and obsessed, he grabbed viciously at the Doctor's throat. Amazingly the frail old man was able to push the younger man away and, still suffering from the effects of the Doctor's drug, Ian fell crashing to the floor.

Massaging his throat, the Doctor staggered over to a chair as Barbara and Susan burst into the room. Barbara took in first the figure of Ian falling senseless to the floor, and then the Doctor, stunned and gasping for breath on a chair.

She rushed over to Ian's side. Susan ran to her grandfather.

'It's no use pretending now!' crowed the Doctor as he got his breath back. 'I was right! It was you all along!'

'Don't just sit there!' cried Barbara, not listening. 'Come over here and help him!'

'Help him?' spluttered the Doctor. 'You saw what he tried to do! He nearly strangled me!'

'I saw nothing!' Barbara snapped back. 'All I can see is that he's fainted . . . just like Susan . . .'

'Susan didn't faint,' retorted the Doctor angrily. 'It was you who told her she did – and I very nearly believed you!'

'What does it matter?'

The Doctor, not as hurt as he would have liked to have made out but merely shaken, stood up with the help of a confused Susan.

'Matter, young lady, matter?' he said with affronted dignity. 'That barbarian down there very nearly strangled me! He's no better than those cavemen we met!'

Barbara was no longer paying any attention to the Doctor's self-righteous prattling. 'But he has fainted,' she repeated. 'Look at him.'

'Oh, he's merely play-acting,' dismissed the Doctor, without bothering to look down at the unconscious schoolteacher.

Barbara looked up seriously, her face set in firm concern. 'Doctor, he *has* fainted and I can't believe he wanted to kill you. Don't you see that something terrible's happening to all of us?'

'Not to me,' countered the Doctor, 'nothing at all has happened to me.'

You stupid old man, can't you see that you're the worst affected of the lot of us! thought Barbara viciously. Lower your idiotic defences for just one minute and see what's happening to us!

'This is undoubtedly a plot between the two of you to get control of my Ship,' the Doctor asserted.

'That isn't true!'

'Can't you see I've found you out?' chuckled the Doctor, highly satisfied with his deductive skills. 'Why don't you just admit it?'

'No, why don't you admit it?' countered Barbara savagely. 'Why don't you admit that you haven't a clue as to what's going on around here, and so to save your own precious self-esteem, you're clutching at straws, shifting the blame onto everyone and everything apart from your own precious self!'

She laughed self-deprecatingly. 'Get control of the Ship! We wouldn't know what to do with it even if we had. If you can't operate your own machine I see absolutely no chance of Ian and myself ever working it!'

The Doctor's face reddened with fury at having his ability to control the TARDIS brought into question once more.

'How dare you!' he exploded. 'I will not tolerate this any longer. I told you I'd treat you as my enemies –'

Susan who had remained quiet up to now, scarcely understanding what had been going on and torn between two conflicting loyalties now spoke up. 'No, Grandfather,' she pleaded.

Slightly taken aback, the Doctor looked down at his granddaughter.

'There is no other way, Susan,' he said imperiously.

'But . . .'

'There is no other way, my child,' insisted the Doctor sternly.

Susan bowed her head in defeat, recognising her grandfather's firmness of purpose.

Down by Barbara's side on the floor Ian was beginning to stir but Barbara continued to look up at the Doctor. 'What are you going to do?' she asked apprehensively.

'That, madam, is my concern.'

Barbara turned back to Ian and shook him. 'Come on, Ian, wake up! For heaven's sake, help me!'

Ian muttered a few indistinct words, and Barbara strained to hear them.

'There is no alternative,' continued the Doctor superiorly. 'Your little antics have endangered all our lives.'

Susan crossed slowly over to Ian and Barbara. She had entered the control room a little after Barbara and had not seen as much as the schoolteacher.

'How did he get like this?' she asked, looking down at Ian.

'It's all a charade,' insisted the Doctor flatly.

Susan repeated her question.

'He went near the control panel . . .' Barbara said slowly, and suddenly realisation dawned. 'Just like . . .'

'Just like me,' finished Susan and looked back to the Doctor. 'Grandfather, it did happen to me,' she said earnestly.

'That's right – you remember now!' interrupted Barbara, delightedly seizing on Susan's words. 'You lost your memory and there was this terrible pain at the back of your neck.'

'Yes, that's true . . .'

'What did you think we'd done?' asked Barbara, 'Hypnotised you? Drugged you? Susan, believe me, we wouldn't do anything like that to you!'

'Wouldn't you now?' asked the Doctor cynically. 'I begin to wonder just what it is you and that young man are not capable of. You break your way into my Ship, sabotage its controls and now you are attempting to divide and conquer. She's trying to poison your mind against me, Susan –'

Just then, Ian tried to sit up, and reached out a hand towards the Doctor.

'Doctor . . . the console . . . stay away . . . the controls are alive . . .' he croaked.

Barbara flashed the Doctor a venomous look. 'You see? He wasn't trying to kill you after all! He was trying to pull you away from the control panel. Don't you see?

He wasn't trying to harm you, he was trying to *help* you – though Heaven knows why!'

For a moment the Doctor appeared shaken, as if the truth of Barbara's arguments was just beginning to filter into his mind. Then Susan went over to him and took his arm gently.

'Grandfather, I do believe them,' she said softly. 'They wouldn't have done all those terrible things you said they would.'

But even his granddaughter's words wouldn't sway the Doctor from his irrational and stubborn belief.

'Whose side are you on, Susan?' he asked coldly. 'Mine or theirs?'

'Can't I be on both?'

The Doctor shook his head. 'Oh, I admit they have been very smart,' he said, but this time his voice didn't quite carry the amount of conviction it had previously.

'No, it's not a question of being smart,' countered Susan firmly.

The Doctor took his granddaughter protectively in his arms. 'Don't you see I won't allow them to hurt you, my child? These humans are very resourceful and cunning – who knows what other schemes they may have devised to harm you? You must realise that I am left with only one recourse. They must be put off my Ship!'

Susan broke away from the Doctor's embrace. 'No, Grandfather, you can't!'

'I can and I must.' The old man's tone was final.

'But you can't open the doors,' protested Barbara. 'The controls are dead!'

'Don't underestimate my powers, young lady!' riposted the Doctor.

'But, Grandfather, you've no way of telling what's

out there now that the scanner isn't working properly,' protested Susan. 'There may be no air; it may be freezing; it might even be too hot to exist . . .'

The Doctor played his master card. 'Yes – or it might be Earth in the twentieth-century. Hasn't that occurred to you? My Ship is very valuable . . .'

'Why are you so suspicious of us?' asked Barbara coldly.

'Put yourself in my place, young lady. You would do precisely the same thing.'

Barbara turned away with a snort of derision; if the Doctor had any sense or understanding of them at all he would know they would never behave in the hysterical and illogical way he was behaving now.

The Doctor looked down dispassionately at Ian. 'It's time to end all your play-acting, Chesterton. You're getting off the Ship!'

'Now?' he asked groggily.

'This instant!'

Too weak to argue, and still dazed, Ian looked up at Barbara. 'You'll have to help me up,' he said pathetically. 'I'll be all right when I'm outside in the fresh air.'

'Grandfather, look at him,' pleaded Susan. 'He doesn't even know what's happening. I won't let you do this.'

The Doctor regarded his granddaughter for a moment, recognising in her the same firmness of purpose which he had always displayed. He knew that she would not weaken in her resolve.

Finally, to save some face he announced: 'Of course, if they would like to confess what they have done to my Ship I might possibly change my mind.' The Doctor began to march over to the lever on the control console which opened the doors.

'Why won't you believe us! We haven't –'

An ominous sound suddenly interrupted Barbara.

It was a low repetitive chime, like the tolling of a huge bronze bell. It seemed to echo from deep within the TARDIS itself, and seemed to infiltrate their very beings.

The Doctor and Susan looked urgently at each other, instantly recognising the sound for what it was. The Doctor instinctively held his granddaughter protectively in his arms.

Ian was filled with a foreboding he had not felt since he was a small child. Barbara was immediately reminded of a verse she had learnt long ago at school and the meaning of which she had never fully understood till this moment: *Ask not for whom the bell tolls, it tolls for thee.*

'What was that?' Ian asked fearfully, as the last reverberating tones echoed away.

'The danger signal . . .' Susan's voice was trembling and her face was deathly white. She clutched at her grandfather's arm. 'It's never sounded before . . .'

'The Fault Locator!' cried the Doctor and rushed over to the bank of instruments at the far end of the control chamber.

Lights were flickering furiously on and off and the VDU screen itself showed a crazy jumble of flashing figures and letters. The entire machine seemed to be overloading; sparks and wisps of acrid smoke filled the entire area beyond the protective glass screen.

'Don't touch it, Doctor!' warned Ian as he staggered to his feet with Barbara's help.

Susan was at the Doctor's side in an instant. She

looked up and recognised the fear in her grandfather's face. It was the most horrifying feeling she had ever had in her life, seeing that look of terror.

'What is it?' she asked, already knowing what the answer would be, but somehow wishing that the Doctor would suddenly turn and tell her that everything was going to be all right. 'Tell me, please . . .'

The Doctor looked down at her and then turned to Ian and Barbara who had joined them in the Fault Locator area.

'The whole of the Fault Locator had just given us a warning,' he announced gravely.

Ian looked at the green VDU screen as it flashed on and off, casting its macabre emerald light on all their faces. It was seemingly registering every single piece of equipment on board the TARDIS.

'But everything can't be wrong!' he said incredulously.

'That is exactly what it says,' said the Doctor. 'Every single machine on board the Ship, down to the very smallest component, is breaking down.' He looked gravely at his companions, as though considering whether to tell them the truth. Finally he decided.

The words came heavy to his lips: 'I'm afraid that the TARDIS is dying . . .'

9

The Brink of Disaster

For minutes all four of the time-travellers stared at each other in dumbstruck horror. It seemed impossible to believe that the machine which had become their sanctuary and only hope of safety in a threatening universe was about to die. It was like being a passenger in an aircraft who has just been told that the plane is about to crash and that there is nothing the pilot can do to prevent it. Like those passengers there could be no escape from the doomed ship.

Finally Ian broke the heavy, doom-laden silence.

'But, Doctor how can that be? How can the Ship just die?'

The Doctor pointed back to the Fault Locator. 'Whenever one small piece of machinery fails a little light illuminates and the fault is registered on that screen. By its very nature the Fault Locator is designed to be free of any malfunction and has a power source separate from the rest of my machine. Now think what would happen if all the lights lit up. It would mean that the Ship is on the point of disintegration!'

He considered Ian and Barbara carefully and then admitted: 'You two are not to blame – all four of us are to blame!'

'That drink you gave us . . .' said Ian.

'A harmless sleeping drug,' admitted the Doctor sheepishly. 'Yes, I rather suspected you were up to some mischief . . .'

Ian nodded. 'I told you not to go near the console. I told you that you might electrocute yourself.'

'I'm afraid I might have misjudged you and Miss Wright,' conceded the Doctor. 'I thought you had sabotaged my Ship in some way. But such damage is far beyond your capabilities. Even I would be incapable of harming the Ship to this degree.'

Susan who had been watching the VDU screen of the Fault Locator as it flashed on and off came back to her grandfather's side. 'It's happening every fifteen seconds,' she said and added, 'I counted the seconds.'

'Very well,' said the Doctor. 'Please go on counting.' As Susan went back to the Fault Locator he turned to the schoolteachers.

'Now, listen very carefully. We are on the brink of disaster; the TARDIS's circuits are failing because of some unknown force. The Ship could fall apart at any moment. We must forget any petty differences we might have and all four of us must work closely together. We must work to find out where we are and what is happening to my Ship. Once we know that there may be the chance of saving ourselves.'

Ian was tempted to say that that was exactly what he and Barbara had been suggesting from the very beginning. Instead he let the Doctor continue.

'The facts are these: there is a strong force at work somewhere which is threatening my Ship, so strong that every piece of equipment is out of action at the same time.'

'The life support systems are still functioning,' pointed out Barbara. Even in the present crisis she could still hear the in-out in-out breathing of the

98

machine which had so terrified her before but was now becoming oddly reassuring, almost like the heartbeat a baby hears in the warm protection of its mother's womb.

'Yes,' said the Doctor, 'and that is most unusual. Why isn't that failing when everything else around us is?'

'It's almost as if whatever force it is wants to keep us alive . . .' Barbara thought aloud, and shivered as she thought for what possible terrifying purpose.

'But you said that nothing could penetrate the TARDIS's defences, Doctor,' Ian remembered.

'Exactly. No evil intelligence can get inside the TARDIS. The Ship is equipped with a very powerful built-in defence mechanism, which among other things protects us from the forces of the time vortex.

'Neither do I believe any longer that either of you are responsible for our predicament. And we haven't crash-landed – I would have discovered that immediately.'

'But what is it then?' asked Ian despairingly.

'I don't know but we must find out soon!'

'Just how long have we got?' asked Barbara.

Susan returned from the Fault Locator. 'The screen is still flashing on and off every quarter of a minute,' she said.

'But what does that prove?' Ian was at a loss to understand.

'That we have a measure of time as long as it lasts,' the Doctor replied cryptically.

He stroked his chin and looked thoughtfully at the melted face of his ormolu clock. Suddenly his eyes flashed with understanding. 'Yes, of course!' he said excitedly. 'That explains the melted clockface!'

'How?' asked Barbara. 'I don't understand.'

'Don't you see?' The Doctor's excitement was obvious as he explained his theory. 'We had time taken away from us' – here he pointed at the clockface, and then indicated the flashing screen of the Fault Locator – 'and now it's being given back to us because it's running out!'

As if in response to his words, the lights in the control room suddenly flashed on, bathing the chamber for a moment in a bright circle of light. A sonorous clanging, lighter in tone and less threatening than the alarm signal, resounded throughout the room. Beneath their feet the floor vibrated slightly, causing the four time-travellers to stagger.

'The column!' cried Susan and pointed to the centre of the control console.

All eyes looked at the time rotor which throughout their ordeal had remained motionless. The complex circuitry within it flashed momentarily and the column itself slowly rose, and then fell back jerkily, stationary again.

'Impossible!' murmured the Doctor to himself. He was visibly shaken.

'Doctor, I thought the column moved when the power was on and we were in flight,' said Ian.

The Doctor nodded. 'That is correct. The very heart of the TARDIS lies directly beneath that column.'

'So what made it move?'

'The source of power,' explained the Doctor. 'The column serves to weigh down and hold that power in check. When the column rises it proves the extent of the power thrust.'

'Then what would have happened if the column had

come out completely?' asked Barbara nervously.

'The power would be free to escape . . .' said Susan slowly, as she realised the horrific implications.

The Doctor stared fascinated at the now motionless column. Compared to this, all the other malfunctions of the TARDIS were just minor irritations. This was much more serious. If the power beneath the column was indeed trying to escape . . .

'Can it be possible that this is the end?' he said aloud to himself.

'The end? What are you talking about?' asked Ian.

The Doctor turned and looked sombrely at his three companions. He put a protective arm around Susan's shoulder.

'I believe that the power which drives my machine is attempting to escape.'

'But that's impossible!' protested Ian fiercely, willing himself not to believe the Doctor. 'We checked the power rooms; everything there was fine.'

The Doctor nodded. 'Nevertheless that is the only explanation,' he said, and continued as if he were addressing a lecture hall of disinterested students: 'The build-up of power will swiftly increase until the surge will be so great that the weight of the time rotor will not be able to contain it.'

'Can you be certain?' asked Barbara weakly.

'As certain as I can be about anything,' said the Doctor.

He looked meaningfully at each of his companions, and announced: 'According to the readings from the Fault Locator we have precisely fifteen minutes in which to survive, or to find an escape from our situation.'

'Fifteen minutes . . .' echoed Ian disbelievingly. He felt oddly detached, as though he were somewhere else, looking down on himself being delivered this cruel sentence of death. 'As little as that?'

'Maybe less . . .' replied the Doctor. 'And now I suggest that we do not waste any more time.'

Leaving his companions standing shocked and speechless, the Doctor crossed over to the control console.

'Be careful, Doctor,' urged Ian, fearful lest the Doctor should receive a shock or something even worse. 'Remember what happened last time.'

The Doctor waved the schoolmaster's concern aside. 'It's quite safe, Chesterton,' he reassured him. 'This is where I stood when I tried the scanner switch.'

Barbara who had moved a little way off from her fellow travellers and had been examining the melted clockface thoughtfully, suddenly spoke up. 'Yes . . . the rest of the control console is electrified. Only that one control panel is perfectly safe. Why should that be?'

'Is that really so important just now, Miss Wright?' asked the Doctor, a little of his former impatience returning.

'Barbara, what do you mean?' asked Ian and looked curiously over at her. He recognised the expression on Barbara's face. It was the same look on many of his pupils' faces when a particularly difficult physics equation suddenly became clear for them: that peculiar mixture of understanding, delight, and amazement that they could have been so stupid for so long.

But Barbara heard neither Ian nor the Doctor. Instead she looked wonderingly around the control room, and for the first time noticed that the solitary shaft of

102

light which bathed the control console did not, in fact, shine centrally down onto the console. Rather it slanted down onto that one particular panel, the panel which contained the scanner switch.

The two major sources of illumination in the control chamber were that beam, and the maddeningly flashing lights from the Fault Locator. She sniffed incredulously to herself and then, frowning, looked at the melted clockface and the shattered remains of her own wristwatch in the corner of the room. She remembered the sequence of images on the scanner, the opening of the exit doors, the strange, poltergeist-like events in the laboratory which prevented her from destroying herself . . .

In the darkness of the control room a light was beginning slowly to dawn in Barbara's mind. She told herself not to be so silly. To apply some logic to the situation.

But things aren't always logical, are they?

Surely it couldn't be? But yes! It was almost as if someone was trying to tell them something . . .

Susan at her grandfather's side was finding it difficult to hold back the tears. 'We're not going to stop it in time, are we, Grandfather?' she moaned disconsolately.

The Doctor shook his head as he cast despairing eyes over the controls and hugged his granddaughter closer. 'I don't even know where to begin, child,' he admitted disarmingly. 'I wish I could offer you more hope but I am at a complete loss. The problem seems to be beyond all logical argument . . .' He clicked his tongue in irritation. 'If only I had some sort of clue . . .'

'Perhaps we've been given nothing else *but* clues . . .'

Everyone turned to look at Barbara.

'What do you mean?' asked Ian. 'Like the food machine registering empty when it wasn't?'

'Yes,' said Barbara slowly as she tried to sort out into some sort of sense the crazy thoughts which were whirring around in her head. 'But the clock is the most important of all – it made us aware of time.'

'By taking time away from us?' asked Susan excitedly, remembering her grandfather's words and strangely intrigued by Barbara's theory.

The schoolteacher nodded. 'And it replaced time by the regular flashing light on the Fault Locator . . .'

'Yes, it did . . .' said Ian, slowly beginning to see what Barbara was getting at. He felt a thrill of excitement down his spine.

'It? It?' snapped the Doctor irritably. 'What do you mean? Who is giving us all these clues?'

'The TARDIS?' ventured Barbara.

'My machine cannot think,' countered the Doctor automatically.

The truth was that the Doctor was so convinced of his own superiority he had never before even considered the matter.

Barbara, who realised how absurd the proposition would sound to someone as logically-minded as the Doctor, tried to soften the idea. 'But the Ship does have a built-in defence mechanism, doesn't it?' she asked reasonably.

'Yes.'

'Well, that's where we've all been wrong all this time. Originally it wasn't the TARDIS that was at fault, it was *us*. We've all been so busy accusing each other, and defending ourselves from each other, that we were ignorant of the real danger. And the TARDIS – or the defence mechanism, whichever you like to call it – has been trying to tell us so ever since!'

The possibility fascinated Ian. 'A machine that can observe, and think for itself . . . Is that feasible, Doctor?'

'Think, as you or I think, Chesterton, that is certainly impossible,' maintained the Doctor. 'But to think as a machine . . . yes, that is a fascinating theory. I must admit to you that there are aspects of my machine which I still don't yet fully understand . . . Yes, yes, it *is* possible!'

'We didn't know it but the TARDIS has, of all things, been looking after us!' said Barbara. 'When Ian got lost in the corridors the TARDIS guided him to the Doctor; when he was trapped in that airless room, it was the TARDIS who unlocked the door for him. It even frightened me half out of my wits in the laboratory and in doing so saved my life!'

'But even if that is so, how can it help us out of our predicament?' the Doctor asked eagerly, for the first time in his life asking someone else's advice.

'You said that the power is stored underneath the column,' continued Barbara. 'What would want to make it escape?'

The Doctor shrugged. 'I've been racking my brains. I simply do not know.'

'Something outside?' suggested Ian.

'Possibly.'

'A magnetic force?'

'It would have to be a strong one to affect the TARDIS,' said the Doctor, 'one at least as strong as that of an entire solar system, probably even a galaxy –'

As if in affirmation the lights of the control chamber

flashed up once more, momentarily blinding them, and the same sonorous clang they had heard before resounded throughout the control room.

'You see!' cried Barbara triumphantly. 'The TARDIS has been trying to warn us all along! The lights in Ian's room waking him up when the Doctor was about to operate the electrified controls. His door being unlocked when he had locked it . . . All those blackouts we had!'

'Yes! But only if we went near the control column!' said Susan.

'They could have been the result of the power escaping,' reasoned Ian.

'No, they couldn't,' stated the Doctor definitely. 'If you had felt the full force of the TARDIS's power, dear boy, you wouldn't be here now to speak of it. So great is the power that you would have been blown to atoms in seconds. Besides, a part of the console is safe . . .'

'But why should just that one panel be safe, and nowhere else?' wondered Barbara. 'What's so special about it? And what did those pictures we saw on the scanner mean? Could it have been some kind of message? Was the TARDIS actually trying to tell us something in the only way it could?'

Again the lights of the control room flashed, and the chamber resounded with a clang of affirmation.

The Doctor was silent for a moment and looked around, not at Susan, Ian and Barbara but rather at the walls and the instrumentation of the TARDIS. There was a look of wonderment in his steel-blue eyes.

'Very well,' he said finally, 'we will try the scanner again – but I warn you, we're clutching at straws.'

He turned to Barbara and Susan. 'Now, I want you

two to stand by the doors. Should they open again I want you to tell me whatever it is you can see outside. Do you understand?'

The girls nodded and crossed over to the large double doors. The Doctor beckoned Ian surreptitiously over to his side by the control console. There was a worried frown on his face. He drew Ian close to him so that only he would hear what he was about to say.

'I lied deliberately so they won't know,' he confided to Ian in a hushed whisper.

'Won't know what?'

'We do not have fifteen minutes left to us; we only have ten. When the end does come Susan and Miss Wright won't know anything about it.'

Ian nodded approvingly. Strangely he no longer felt any panic or fear, merely a calm and resigned acceptance of the facts. 'There's no hope then?' he asked.

The Doctor shook his head. 'I can't see any,' he replied. 'If only we had heeded these warnings earlier, or stopped bickering among ourselves perhaps . . . But now, I'm afraid not. Will you face it with me?'

'What are you two talking about?' Susan called from the other end of the room.

'Oh, just a theory of mine which didn't work,' lied Ian.

'Yes, we must solve this problem, you know . . ' said the Doctor with affected confidence. 'Now you two just watch the doors and we'll be out of this mess in no time . . .'

10

A Race against Time

With a trembling hand the Doctor operated the scanner control. All eyes were fixed anxiously on the scanner screen.

For a heart-stopping few seconds, which to the four doomed travellers seemed like hours, nothing happened. Ian and the Doctor looked nervously at each other. Had even the scanner screen with its strange sequence of images broken down too? Then finally – thankfully – the screen on the far wall flickered into life.

Once again the picture of the Malvern Hills appeared, accompanined by the sound of birdsong. The Doctor and Ian looked expectantly over at Barbara and Susan by the doors. Slowly the doors opened, and the same searing white light flooded the control room once more.

Shielding their eyes from the glare Barbara and Susan peered out through the open doors.

'There's nothing there, Grandfather, nothing at all!' cried Susan, a touch of hysteria in her voice. 'It's just a wide, gaping, empty void!'

Slowly the doors closed again and thudded shut. They all looked at the screen. As they expected, it was now showing a picture of the jungle world of Quinnius. Barbara and Susan came over to join the two men.

'Barbara could be right, Doctor, it could be some sort of messsage,' said Ian.

'I *am* right!' retorted Barbara. 'You know I am. When the scanner shows us a good picture like the Malverns the doors open because it should be safe for us to go outside. Then it shows us a terrible picture and the doors close again.'

'But if it is a message what does this mean?' asked the Doctor and pointed to the scanner, where the picture of Quinnius had faded to be replaced by the unidentified planet turning in space. 'After Earth and Quinnius we have this sequence: a planet; a planet in a solar system, getting further and further away; and then a blinding flashing light!'

'And total destruction,' added Barbara, and turned her eyes away from the glare of the scanner screen. 'Unless . . .' She drew her companions' attentions to the closed double doors. 'If I'm right, the doors are shut because what is outside now is hostile to us . . . Were the other pictures just clues? Could that picture on the scanner now be what's outside the Ship? Could that be the danger?'

The Doctor's eyes suddenly blazed with understanding. He clapped his hands together in satisfaction.

'Of course!' he cried triumphantly. 'It's all clear to me now: the pictures on the screen, everything! It's our journey – our journey to destruction!'

'Hang on,' said Ian. 'You mean to say that we are heading on a course straight to that explosion?'

'Yes,' said Barbara. 'And the TARDIS refused to destroy itself – so the defence mechanism stopped the Ship and it's been trying to tell us so ever since!'

'Exactly!' said the Doctor. 'The TARDIS is ultimately unable to resist the overwhelming forces of that explosion; but it has stalled itself in the void, trying to delay for as long as possible that fatal moment when it must be finally and irrevocably destroyed!'

The affirming clang which echoed throughout the room now was almost deafening. The floor beneath their feet shuddered violently, sending the four companions staggering off in all directions.

'I know now,' cried the Doctor, as he leant against the safe part of the control console for support, 'I know!' He turned everyone's gaze towards the scanner screen: the final sequence was repeating itself over and over again.

'I said it would take at the very least the force of an entire solar system to attract the power away from my Ship. And that is exactly what is happening! We have arrived at the very beginning of all things!

'Outside the Ship, hydrogen atoms are rushing towards each other, fusing, coalescing, until minute little collections of matter are created. And so the process will go on and on for millions of years until dust is formed. The dust then will eventually become solid entity – the birth of new suns and new planets. The mightiest force in the history of creation beyond which the TARDIS cannot pass!'

'You don't mean the Big Bang?' asked Barbara incredulously.

'No,' said the Doctor. 'I doubt whether even my machine would be capable of withstanding as well as it has done the forces generated by the creation of the entire Universe; but the creation of a galaxy – of your galaxy – of the Milky Way!'

'But, Doctor, how did we get here?' asked Ian. 'When we left the planet Skaro where did you ask the TARDIS to take us?' The Doctor hesitated. 'Think, Doctor, think!' he urged.

The Doctor paused for a moment. 'I had hoped to reach your planet Earth in the twentieth-century,' the old man said. 'Skaro was in the future and so I used the Fast Return switch.'

'The Fast Return switch? What's that?'

'It's a means whereby the TARDIS is supposed to retrace its previous journeys.'

'What do you mean "supposed to"?' asked Barbara.

'Exactly what I say, young lady,' snapped the Doctor. 'I've never used it before!'

'Don't you see, Doctor, you've sent us back too far! We've gone back past the Earth of 1963, we've even gone on back past prehistoric times!' Ian seized the old man by the shoulders. 'Doctor, show me that switch! Where is it?'

The Doctor peered down at the control console. 'I can't very well see it in this light,' he flustered.

'It's near the scanner switch,' volunteered Susan.

'Of course!' said Barbara. 'The one part of the control console that the TARDIS kept safe for us! Only we were too stupid to realise!'

'Doctor, hurry – we can't have much time left!' Ian reminded him.

'There! That's the one,' said the Doctor and pointed down to a small, square-shaped button on one of the keyboards of the control panel.

'So how does it work?' Ian asked urgently.

'You merely press it down and –' The Doctor caught his breath as he examined the switch. 'It's stuck! I pressed it down and it hasn't released itself!'

'You mean it's been on all this time?'

'Yes, it must have been.'

'Well, don't just stand there! Get it unstuck!'

From out of his pockets the Doctor took a small screwdriver. Frantically he began to unscrew the panel which contained the keyboard. Around him Ian, Barbara and Susan watched with anxious eyes, holding their breath as the Doctor's aged fingers fumbled with the screwdriver.

Finally the Doctor lifted up the panel and poked around in the interior workings of the mechanism. He jerked quickly with the screwdriver at the jammed button and with the most anxiously awaited *click!* in history, the control released itself.

Like an old, forgotten friend the lights returned to the TARDIS control chamber, dispelling instantly the black shadows and illuminating the drawn and weary faces of the four exhausted time-travellers. The TARDIS hummed almost joyously into life again, and in the centre of the control console the time rotor resumed its stately rise and fall.

Close to collapse, Barbara threw herself gratefully into a chair and Ian clasped her hand firmly in support. By the console Susan hugged her grandfather and finally let flow the tears she had held back for so long.

Released from their terrible nightmare at last everyone breathed a heartfelt sigh of relief.

For a long time no one said a word.

Epilogue

It was Susan who finally broke the silence. 'Are you sure we're safe now, Grandfather?' she asked.

The Doctor smiled affectionately down at her. 'Yes, we can all relax now. But I must say that it was a very narrow escape, a very narrow escape indeed. We've all been very lucky.'

'So what happened?'

The Doctor explained to her the reason for the TARDIS's disability.

Susan was puzzled. 'But why didn't the Fault Locator tell us what the problem was?'

'Elementary, my child,' said the Doctor. 'The Fault Locator is designed to identify faults in the TARDIS's machinery; the smallest imaginable thing can go wrong with my Ship and the Fault Locator will identify it. But the Fast Return switch wasn't broken – it was merely stuck! That's why the Fault Locator couldn't register it. It's as simple as that!

'You know, I should have thought of that myself at the very beginning. I think your old grandfather is going a tiny bit round the bend!' The Doctor chuckled and then his face turned serious. He hugged Susan even tighter. 'And I think you were very brave, Susan. I was proud of you.'

Susan smiled gratefully at the Doctor. 'But what about all these warnings we had?' she asked. 'The lights, the control panels . . . was it really the TARDIS warning us? Can it really think and act for itself?'

The Doctor smiled and then sighed once more. 'I truly don't know, my child. But as we travel on our journeys I feel I am learning more and more about my machine. There were times on our travels, I don't mind admitting to you now, when I felt that we were never quite alone . . .'

Susan smiled and then directed her grandfather's attention to Ian and Barbara who were at the other end of the room. Barbara was sitting in the chair, her arms folded and her face set hard. Ian was talking softly to her.

'Grandfather, what about them?' Susan asked in a whisper. 'What about Ian and Barbara?'

'What about them?' asked the Doctor diffidently.

'You said some terrible things about them,' continued Susan. 'When I thought Ian was going to attack you even I was against him . . . But we misjudged them. All through this terrible thing all they've wanted to do was help us . . . Don't you think you really ought to apologise to them?'

The Doctor's eyes flashed with anger for a moment at the very idea; apologies were only for people who had been proved wrong, and the Doctor was never wrong. But his granddaughter reminded him of the manner in which he had treated his two human companions and the debt he owed to both of them – especially Barbara. And then he flushed as he realised that he had indeed been proven wrong.

'Please, Grandfather, make it up to them,' she urged once more. 'It's not so much to ask for, is it? And we've all got to live together after all . . .'

The Doctor scratched his chin thoughtfully and then to Susan's delight wandered over to the two schoolteachers. He tried – unsuccessfully – to affect an air of nonchalance.

'Well . . . I . . . er . . . er . . .' he began.

Ian turned to him and smiled. He raised a hand to stem the Doctor's awkward words. 'Don't bother to say a thing, Doctor,' he said magnanimously. 'You know, there are times when I can read every thought on your face . . .'

The Doctor turned an even brighter shade of red.

'Er . . . yes . . . well, thank you, Chesterton. I always did think you were a man without any recrimination in you.' The Doctor ventured a comradely pat on the younger man's back. To his surprise, he discovered that it wasn't hard to do at all, and the young man returned it.

You see, Grandfather, thought Susan and smiled, *it isn't so difficult after all*.

The Doctor turned his attention to Barbara. She was still sitting in the chair, staring thoughtfully into space. Her ordeal had held back her tears but now it was over they were beginning to form at the corners of her eyes. Ian and Susan tactfully drew away as the old man approached Barbara.

'I . . . er, I feel I owe you an apology, Miss Wright . . .' the Doctor began falteringly.

Barbara arched an eyebrow in interest and surprise as the Doctor continued: 'You were absolutely right all along – and it was me who was wrong, I freely admit it. It was your instinct against my logic and you triumphed. The blackouts, the still pictures, and the clock – you read a story into them and you were de-

117

termined to hold to it . . . Miss Wright, we owe you our lives.'

Barbara regarded the Doctor. The look in her eyes told him that his apology wasn't enough. 'You said some terrible things to me and Ian,' she reminded him.

The Doctor lowered his head in agreement. 'Yes, and I unreservedly apologise for them. I suppose it's the injustice. When I made that threat to put you off the Ship, it must have affected you deeply.'

Barbara laughed ironically. 'What do you care what I think or feel?'

'As we learn about each other on our travels so we learn about ourselves.'

'Perhaps.'

'No, certainly,' insisted the Doctor softly. 'Because I accused you injustly you were determined to prove me wrong. You put your mind to the problem and you solved it . . . As you said before, we are together now whether we like it or not. Susan and I need you and Chesterton, just as much as you need us. We may have originally been unwilling fellow travellers but I hope that from now on we may be something more to each other. There is a boundless universe out there beyond your wildest dreams, Miss Wright, a thousand lives to lead, and a myriad worlds of unimaginable wonders to explore. Let us explore them together not in anger and resentment, but in friendship.' He looked expectantly at her and offered her his hand. 'Miss Wright? . . . Barbara?'

To his delight, Barbara smiled and shook his hand. Watching from a distance, Ian and Susan winked happily at each other.

Conclusion

Yawning, Barbara walked into the control room to find the Doctor scanning the read-outs and graphic displays on the control console. In the centre of the console the time rotor was slowly falling to a welcome halt. The deafening crescendo of dematerialisation began to fill the control chamber.

Swiftly, the Doctor's hands flickered over the controls as he brought the time-machine into a safe landing. He examined the atmospheric readings which were displayed on one of the control boards.

'A perfect landing,' he said as he became aware of Barbara's presence. 'How did you sleep, my dear?'

'Like a log,' smiled Barbara.

'Quite understandable too after your ordeal.'

'So what's it like outside, Doctor?' she asked.

'Normal Earth gravity and the air is remarkably unpolluted,' the Doctor replied, 'although it is a trifle chilly. I suggest you go off and find yourself a warm coat – we must look after you, you know.'

Barbara nodded and went off in the direction of the TARDIS's extensive wardrobe.

'So where are we then, Doctor?' asked Ian who had just walked into the control room with Susan after having breakfast.

The Doctor looked shocked. 'Goodness gracious, you surely don't expect me to know that, do you!'

Ian burst into a fit of uncontrollable giggles.

'My dear boy, what on Earth are you laughing at?' spluttered the Doctor. 'Really there are times when I find it quite impossible to understand either you or your companion!'

He smiled and, to his surprise, found that Ian smiled back. As Barbara came back, wearing a long overcoat, and loaded with warm clothing for all of them, he operated the door controls. The double doors buzzed slowly open.

A brisk refreshing wind rushed into the control room. Beyond the double doors the four companions could see an infinite expanse of snow and white-capped mountains set against a breathtakingly blue sky. It was one of the most awe-inspiring and beautiful sights any of them had ever seen.

'Well, shall we go out?' the Doctor asked his friends.

Barbara smiled and took the Doctor's outstretched arm. Susan and Ian followed.

Looking out over the mountains, Barbara had to agree that the Doctor had been right – there were indeed a myriad wonderful sights to see in the wide Universe.

If they were truthful with themselves, Ian and Barbara had to admit that they were finally beginning to enjoy their travels with the Doctor in the TARDIS. Smiling to each other, they recalled that far-away foggy November night.

It had all started in a junkyard. Who could say where it would end?

DOCTOR WHO

0426114558	TERRANCE DICKS **Doctor Who –** **Abominable Snowmen**	£1.35
0426203054	**Doctor Who–Ambassadors** **of Death**	£1.95
0426200373	**Doctor Who – Android Invasion**	£1.25
0426201086	**Doctor Who – Androids of Tara**	£1.95
0426193423	**Doctor Who – Arc of Infinity**	£1.35
0426202538	PAUL ERIKSON **Dr Who – The Ark**	£1.75
0426116313	IAN MARTER **Doctor Who – Ark in Space**	£1.95
0426201043	TERRANCE DICKS **Doctor Who –** **Armageddon Factor**	£1.50
0426112954	**Doctor Who – Auton Invasion**	£1.50
0426201582	ERIC PRINGLE **Doctor Who – The Awakening**	£1.50
0426195884	JOHN LUCAROTTI **Doctor Who – The Aztecs**	£1.50
0426202546	TERENCE DUDLEY **Dr Who – Black Orchid**	£1.75
042620123X	DAVID FISHER **Doctor Who –** **Creature from the Pit**	£1.95
0426113160	DAVID WHITAKER **Doctor Who – Crusaders**	£1.50
0426116747	TERRANCE DICKS **Doctor Who – Brain of Morbius**	£1.95
0426110250	**Doctor Who –** **Carnival of Monsters**	£1.50*

DOCTOR WHO

0426193261	CHRISTOPHER H. BIDMEAD **Doctor Who – Castrovalva**	£1.50
0426199596	TERRANCE DICKS **Doctor Who – The Caves of Androzani**	£1.50
042611471X	MALCOLM HULKE **Doctor Who – Cave Monsters**	£1.50
0426202511	G. DAVIS & A. BINGEMAN **Dr Who – The Celestial Toymaker**	£1.60
0426117034	TERRANCE DICKS **Doctor Who – Claws of Axos**	£1.50
0426114981	BRIAN HAYLES **Doctor Who – Curse of Peladon**	£1.50
0426114639	GERRY DAVIS **Doctor Who – Cybermen**	£1.50
0426113322	BARRY LETTS **Doctor Who – Daemons**	£1.50
0426101103	DAVID WHITAKER **Doctor Who – Daleks**	£1.50
042611244X	TERRANCE DICKS **Doctor Who – Dalek Invasion of Earth**	£1.50
0426103807	**Doctor Who – Day of The Daleks**	£1.35
0426119657	**Doctor Who – Deadly Assassin**	£1.50
042620042X	**Doctor Who – Death to The Daleks**	£1.35
0426200969	**Doctor Who – Destiny of the Daleks**	£1.50

DOCTOR WHO

	MALCOLM HULKE	
0426108744	**Doctor Who –** **Dinosaur Invasion**	**£1.35**
	IAN MARTER	
0426195531	**Doctor Who – The Dominators**	**£1.50**
	MALCOLM HULKE	
0426103726	**Doctor Who –** **Doomsday Weapon**	**£1.50**
	IAN MARTER	
0426193776	**Doctor Who – Earthshock**	**£1.35**
0426201264	**Doctor Who –** **Enemy of the World**	**£1.50**
	BARBARA CLEGG	
042619537X	**Doctor Who – Enlightenment**	**£1.50**
0426202945	**Dr Who – The Faceless Ones**	**£1.75**
	TERRANCE DICKS	
0426200063	**Doctor Who – Face of Evil**	**£1.50**
0426193342	**Doctor Who – Four to Doomsday**	**£1.95**
0426195108	**Doctor Who – The** **Five Doctors**	**£1.75**
	CHRISTOPHER H. BIDMEAD	
0426197801	**Doctor Who – Frontios**	**£1.50**
	ANDREW SMITH	
0426201507	**Doctor Who – Full Circle**	**£1.50**
	VICTOR PEMBERTON	
0426202597	**Dr Who – Fury from the Deep**	**£1.95**
	WILLIAM EMMS	
0426202023	**Dr Who – Galaxy Four**	**£1.60**
	TERRANCE DICKS	
0426112601	**Doctor Who –** **Genesis of the Daleks**	**£1.35**
0426112792	**Doctor Who – Giant Robot**	**£1.95**
	MALCOLM HULKE	
0426115430	**Doctor Who – Green Death**	**£1.50**

DOCTOR WHO

0426201957	DONALD COTTON Doctor Who – The Gunfighters	£1.60
0426200330	TERRANCE DICKS Doctor Who – Hand of Fear	£1.95
0426196767	GERRY DAVIS Doctor Who – The Highlanders	£1.50
0426201310	TERRANCE DICKS Doctor Who – Horns of Nimon	£1.95
0426200098	Doctor Who – Horror of Fang Rock	£1.95
0426108663	BRIAN HAYLES Doctor Who – Ice Warriors	£1.95
0426200772	TERRANCE DICKS Doctor Who – Image of The Fendahl	£1.95
0426196171	Doctor Who – Inferno	£1.50
0426201698	IAN MARTER Doctor Who – The Invasion	£1.50
0426200934	TERRANCE DICKS Doctor Who – Invasion of Time	£1.35
0426200543	Doctor Who – Invisible Enemy	£1.95
0426201485	Doctor Who – Keeper of Traken	£1.95
0426201256	PHILIP HINCHCLIFFE Doctor Who – Keys of Marinus	£1.95
0426195299	TERRANCE DICKS Doctor Who – Kinda	£1.35
0426202279	TERENCE DUDLEY Dr Who – The King's Demons	£1.60
0426203097	Doctor Who – K9 and Company	£1.95
0426201892	TERRANCE DICKS Doctor Who – The Krotons	£1.50*

DOCTOR WHO

0426201477	**DAVID FISHER** **Doctor Who – Leisure Hive**	£1.95
0426110412	**TERRANCE DICKS** **Doctor Who –** **Loch Ness Monster**	£1.60
0426201493	**CHRISTOPHER H. BIDMEAD** **Doctor Who – Logopolis**	£1.35
0426203070	**I. STUART BLACK** **Doctor Who Macra Terror**	£1.95
0426199677	**JOHN LUCAROTTI** **Doctor Who – Marco Polo**	£1.50
0426202325	**PIP & JANE BAKER** **Dr Who – The Mark of the Rani**	£1.60
0426118936	**PHILIP HINCHCLIFFE** **Doctor Who –** **Masque of Mandragora**	£1.95
042620297X	**JOHN LUCAROTTI** **Doctor Who The Massacre**	£1.95
0426193938	**PETER GRIMWADE** **Doctor Who – Mawdryn Undead**	£1.35
0426201361	**TERRANCE DICKS** **Doctor Who – Meglos**	£1.95
0426201663	**Doctor Who – Mind of Evil**	£1.50
0426202864	**PETER LING** **Doctor Who – The Mind Robbers**	£1.75
0426201329	**Doctor Who –** **Monster of Peladon**	£1.95
0426116909	**Doctor Who – Mutants**	£1.95

DOCTOR WHO

0426203194	TERRANCE DICKS **Doctor Who Mysterious Planet**	£1.99
0426201701	DONALD COTTON **Doctor Who – The Mythmakers**	£1.50
0426201302	TERRANCE DICKS **Doctor Who – Nightmare of Eden**	£1.95
0426112520	**Doctor Who – Planet of the Daleks**	£1.95
0426116828	**Doctor Who – Planet of Evil**	£1.95
0426199405	PETER GRIMWADE **Doctor Who – Planet of Fire**	£1.50
0426106555	TERRANCE DICKS **Doctor Who – Planet of the Spiders**	£1.35
0426201019	**Doctor Who – Power of Kroll**	£1.50
0426116666	**Doctor Who – Pyramids of Mars**	£1.35
0426114981	**Doctor Who – Revenge of the Cybermen**	£1.95
0426200926	IAN MARTER **Doctor Who – Ribos Operation**	£1.50
0426202643	**Doctor Who Reign of Terror**	£1.95
0426203089	**Doctor Who The Rescue**	£1.95
0426200616	TERRANCE DICKS **Doctor Who – Robots of Death**	£1.95
0426202880	DONALD COTTON **Doctor Who – The Romans**	£1.95

DOCTOR WHO

0426202309	IAN STUART BLACK **Dr Who – The Savages**	£1.60
042611308X	MALCOLM HULKE **Doctor Who – Sea Devils**	£1.35
0426116585	PHILIP HINCHCLIFFE **Doctor Who – Seeds of Doom**	£1.95
042620252X	TERRANCE DICKS **Dr Who – Seeds of Death**	£1.60
0426202953	NIGEL ROBINSON **Doctor Who The Sensorites**	£1.95
0426202635	ERIC SAWARD **Dr Who – Slipback**	£1.75
0426194578	TERRANCE DICKS **Doctor Who – Snakedance**	£1.35
0426200497	IAN MARTER **Doctor Who – Sontaran Experiment**	£1.95
0426202899	GLYN JONES **Dr Who – The Space Museum**	£1.80
0426110331	MALCOLM HULKE **Doctor Who – Space War**	£1.95
0426201337	TERRANCE DICKS **Doctor Who – State of Decay**	£1.95
0426200993	**Doctor Who – Stones of Blood**	£1.95
0426200594	**Doctor Who – Sunmakers**	£1.50
0426119738	**Doctor Who – Talons of Weng Chiang**	£1.95
0426110684	GERRY DAVIS **Doctor Who – Tenth Planet**	£1.50
0426193857	JOHN LYDECKER **Doctor Who – Terminus**	£1.50

ORDER FORM

STAR BOOKS are obtainable from many booksellers and newsagents. If you have any difficulty list the titles you want and fill in the form below:

<u>TITLE</u>   <u>PRICE</u>

_____

_____

_____

_____

_____

_____

Name _____

Address _____

_____